SBN 361 02112 7
Copyright © 1972 Walt Disney Productions
Published by Purnell Books, Berkshire House,
Queen Street, Maidenhead, Berks.
Reprinted 1973 (twice), 1974, 1975, 1977, 1978
Made and printed in Great Britain by Purnell and Sons Ltd.
Paulton (Bristol) and London

WALT DISNEY'S
GIANT
book of
BEDTIME STORIES

Purnell

CONTENTS

The Tail of a Tiger

SHERE KHAN THE TIGER was angry. He was often bad-tempered—but this time he was angry. And an angry Shere Khan was a sight to see.

His striped tail swished to and fro as he rippled through the jungle. His teeth flashed like white swords as he snarled his anger.

Pity any animal who got in his way!

Why was he so angry?

Once again he had been tricked by Mowgli the Man Cub. So . . . as I said before . . . he was angry. And if you thought that loud noise was Shere Khan purring you ought to listen again: he was grumbling loudly to himself.

Shere Khan was looking for trouble.

He found it.

There in his path was trouble. It was a mongoose. They are small animals with beady eyes who love to fight snakes. They are afraid of nothing—not even angry tigers.

This mongoose was called Marty and he was right in Shere Khan's path.

"Out of my way!" snarled Shere Khan.

Marty's beady eyes shone brightly.

"Don't be so rude," he said.

"Out of my way, small fry," said Shere Khan, his snarl becoming a roar of rage.

"Shan't," said Marty, cheekily.

There was a dull thud. Shere Khan had brought his heavy paw down like a striped hammer, intending to crush the mongoose. But the mongoose had skipped out of the way.

"What a big bully you are!" said the mongoose.

In the trees overhead the monkeys stopped their chattering. The brightly-coloured birds stopped twittering. All the jungle seemed to hold its breath.

Shere Khan poised himself to spring. His weight alone would have flattened Marty the mongoose. Shere Khan sprang. The ground shook as he landed. But Marty was not there.

Shere Khan blinked. He sat back on his haunches and looked around. Where *was* the mongoose?

Then he felt a sharp pain … in his tail.

There was Marty, his teeth sunk deep into Shere Khan's tail—as though it were a snake.

Shere Khan swished his tail backwards and forwards, trying to shake off the mongoose. But one thing Marty had learned about fighting snakes was never to let go.

He did not let go.

With another roar, Shere Khan tried to grab Marty between his huge jaws. It was impossible. He could never get any nearer Marty, because he could never reach his own tail. It was impossible.

Soon Shere Khan was running round in circles. In the trees the monkeys and the brightly-coloured birds started laughing at the mighty Shere Khan, running round in circles chasing his own tail.

Shere Khan stopped running at last. He was dizzy. He was no longer roaring, he was panting.

Marty mongoose took his teeth out of the tiger's tail and walked up to Shere Khan.

"Never, never try to bully anyone smaller than yourself," said Marty. "You never know just what they can do."

And he reached up, tweaked Shere Khan's whiskers and walked off into the jungle.

Shere Khan sat watching him. Then, still panting, he resumed his walk.

Do you know something? He was angrier than ever.

Alice and The Puff Clock

AFTER HER ADVENTURES in Wonderland, Alice was sitting by the river. The river rippled and sang over stones and between its leafy banks.

What the river sang was a lullaby and by and by Alice felt herself drifting off to sleep.

The river sang and Alice slept. This time she did not dream about going to Wonderland or peeping behind the Looking Glass. She dreamed that she had no dreams at all.

And she woke up with a start.

"Oh, dear," she said, "I wonder what the time is. I don't want to be late for tea."

But she had forgotten the little watch that she always carried.

"I'll tell you the time," said a small dandelion at her side. The dandelion had shed his yellow flower and was now a white gossamer ball on a green stem.

"Blow me and the number of breaths it takes to get rid of all my gossamer is the time it is. Two breaths—two o'clock. Three breaths—three o'clock."

Alice picked up the dandelion and blew.

"What's the time?" she asked.

But with her breath all the gossamer lifted into the air, as though it were snowing tiny parachutes. Each parachute carried a dandelion seed. And each seed giggled at their joke:

"The time? The time? It's time for us to go!"

And they whirled away into the air like a blizzard.

Then Alice woke up. Because she had only been dreaming that she had not been dreaming.

"Well I *do* know the time," she said. "I'm hungry. So it must be time for tea."

And she went for tea.

The Wind

THE WIND ROARED. Like a tiger it moved around the house, snarling at the windows and growling down the chimney.

Any moment it seemed as though it would break into the house.

Donald Duck's nephews were scared. They sat up in bed, unable to sleep. And the wind roared.

Donald came in to see them and they told him they were scared.

"The wind seems so angry," they said.

"He's not angry," said Donald. "He's just letting you know that he's there.

"You see, when it's a calm, quiet day the wind gets bored. He sits up there in the clouds and feels that people have forgotten all about him.

"So on a night like this he comes down and pushes the air about a bit, shouting just to make sure that you haven't forgotten him.

"I'm here!" he's bawling. "Can you hear me?

"He doesn't mean any harm by it. But sometimes you're a bit rowdy just like him. You have to let people know that you're still around.

"Just like the wind. And, really you know, he's not roaring, he's laughing."

Then Donald tucked them up in bed and turned out the lights.

The wind outside wasn't really roaring. He was laughing at the windows, chuckling down the chimney.

He was still enjoying the joke when the nephews fell asleep.

By Jiminy! Where's Jiminy?

IT ALL BEGAN when Pinocchio said: "I'm fed up with you, Jiminy! Go away!"

Pinocchio was the wooden puppet, who had been brought to life. Jiminy Cricket was supposed to look after him. Jiminy Cricket was his conscience—his guide through life.

And Pinocchio had just had about enough of Jiminy. He was always interfering. Always telling Pinocchio what was the *right* thing to do.

Like now.

Pinocchio had drunk three milk-shakes and was asking for a fourth at the drugstore when bright little Jiminy popped

up and waved his small umbrella in Pinocchio's face.

"I shouldn't have any more, Pinocchio," he had said. "You'll be ill."

"But I want another one," said Pinocchio.

"Take my word for it . . ." said Jiminy.

But Pinocchio had just about had enough. That's when he said: "I'm fed up with you, Jiminy! Go away!"

Pinocchio ordered his milk-shake, drank it and then looked round to take Jiminy home with him.

But there was no Jiminy Cricket. Nobody to whistle that merry tune as they walked home together, hand in hand.

Suddenly Pinocchio was worried.

"Oh, dear, I wonder if he took me seriously," said Pinocchio. "I didn't really mean for him to go away."

He rushed out of the drug-store. Outside there was a sly, old fox. When Pinocchio asked him where Jiminy had gone the fox said he thought that the little cricket had gone towards the river...

"But why bother about him?" said the fox. "Wouldn't you rather come to my carnival? It's gay! It's mad! It's amusing!"

For the moment Pinocchio was tempt-

13

ed. But then he felt that fourth milkshake rumble in his tummy—and he knew that Jiminy had been right. Jiminy was *always* right.

Pinocchio had to bring him back.

So he rushed away from the fox and towards the river.

It had grown quite dark now. The trees overhanging the water bristled like strange animals. The wind whipped the river into a torrent of fast-moving foam.

A late-working beaver looked up from building his dam.

"Hard work in this weather," said the beaver.

"Yes," said Pinocchio, breathlessly. "Have you seen Jiminy Cricket? He wears a small frock coat, a top hat and carries an umbrella . . ."

"Yes! Yes!" snapped the beaver. "No need to give me his case history. If you mean that whistling cricket, he got into one of the boats for hire, that go on the river, about a half-hour ago or more.

"Come to think of it. I haven't seen him for some time."

The beaver looked up at the sky.

"He shouldn't be out on the river in this weather. Blowing up quite a storm," he said.

Pinocchio ran in the direction the beaver pointed out. And ran and ran.

"Jiminy!" he called as he ran. "Jiminy!"

There was no answer but the gathering moan of the wind.

Breathless, Pinocchio still ran on. Roots of trees grabbed at his feet trying to trip him up. Brambles clung to his hair trying to pull him back.

"Jiminy!"

Then Pinocchio saw him.

Out there on the fast-flowing river was Jiminy Cricket, trying to row his tiny boat—against the current. Ahead were the rapids!

Pinocchio knew what would happen if

the fragile boat got caught up in the rapids. It would be smashed to matchwood! And Jiminy . . . ! Pinocchio shuddered to think . . .

He called again. Jiminy turned his face towards the bank and saw Pinocchio.

He called back to Pinocchio, but the words were whipped out of his mouth.

Pinocchio did not call out any more. He plunged out into the river to rescue his little friend.

It was only when he got into the river that he remembered. He could not swim.

He felt that there was no ground beneath his feet. His mouth was full of water. His head went under.

Beneath the surface the water was calm. A fish went swimming by, looking at him strangely. Then Pinocchio jerked his head up again. He felt something hooked on to his collar.

It was the handle of Jiminy's umbrella. With a mighty effort Jiminy pulled Pinocchio to the side of the bank, guiding his boat with his other hand.

Gulping and gasping Pinocchio and Jiminy lay on the bank, watching the river flow perilously on.

"Thanks for trying to rescue me," said Jiminy.

"Thanks for rescuing me," said Pinocchio.

"Shucks!" said Jiminy. "Seeing you in the water gave me the strength to beat that dang awful river. When a friend's in need you gotta give all you've got."

"I'll always listen to what you say in future," said Pinocchio.

"Uh! Uh!" said Jiminy. "I'll believe that when it happens."

"Now let's go and have a milk-shake to celebrate," said Pinocchio.

"Same old Pinocchio," said Jiminy Cricket.

And he laughed.

The Tramp and The Bone

THE TRAMP WAS ON THE PROWL. The Tramp was a bristly-haired mongrel whose bravery was as high as his pedigree was low. He was always on the run from the people at the Dog Pound. But he didn't mind. He liked a bit of adventure.

And he was prowling now, looking for some food. He hadn't eaten for a day—not since that night he invaded the chicken house—and his tummy rumbled to remind him that he ought to be getting some food into it before long.

So The Tramp sniffed his way along the sidewalk, keeping a wary eye open for those Dog Pound people.

Then his nose told him that he was near some very good food indeed. He was just outside a butcher's.

And there, sitting high on the butcher's slab, was a large beautiful bone.

It was a giant of a bone. It dripped with juice, and smelled like heaven!

The Tramp went into the shop cautiously. Behind the cash register was a man, who didn't seem to be taking any notice of him.

The Tramp reached up a paw to grab the bone when—

"GET OUT OF IT, YOU PESKY MUTT!"

It was the man behind the cash register. He had a thin, rat-like face and his eyes glittered with rage as he saw The Tramp.

The Tramp ran out of the shop, deciding that retreat was not necessarily surrender.

He stood outside the shop. The man remained where he was. The Tramp thought: "I'll show him!" Defiantly, The Tramp howled.

He made such a racket that people stopped in the street to wonder what was wrong.

Then The Tramp saw a big fat man running towards him and the shop.

The man wore a straw boater and a striped apron and he was shouting as he ran: "What's wrong?"

The man ran into the shop and saw the other man behind the cash register.

Then what a surprise!

The rat-faced man, whom The Tramp thought was the butcher, came running out of the shop pursued by the big, fat man.

The big, fat man stopped, red of face, just outside the shop while the other man ran off into the distance.

"Good boy!" said the man, who was really the butcher. "You just stopped him from robbing me. He was opening my cash register. How about a reward, eh?"

And he handed The Tramp down that luscious, juicy bone that he had been eyeing so hungrily.

"Perhaps you'd like to stay here for the night," said the butcher. "Seems to me that I need a good guard-dog."

The Tramp curled up at the back of the shop. He didn't think that he'd stay there. He was too restless, ever to stay in one place at a time.

But he appreciated the offer. And it was pleasant to relax and not to worry about danger.

Then, as he gnawed at that delicious bone, he thought happily: "It all goes to prove that honesty really is the best policy!"

The Glass Slipper

AND THEY ALL LIVED happily ever after.

I mean Prince Charming and Cinderella. But that isn't the end of the story, by any manner of means. Oh, dear, no!

For instance, whatever happened to that glass slipper that fitted Cinderella so neatly and made Prince Charming ask her to be his bride?

I'll let you into a secret. They threw it away.

They had a perfectly good reason for doing so. Both the Prince and Cinderella had been told by the Fairy Godmother that it would be lucky for them to throw it into the river and make a wish.

So that is what they did. They threw it into the river, made a wish that they would live happily ever after, and the glass slipper sank down into the water to the amazement and surprise of the fish who were swimming there.

And there it stayed for a long, long time.

Until one day Mole was out fishing on the river, in his little boat. Both the Water Rat and Toad of Toad Hall, his best friends, had gone away for the day on business.

So, to cheer himself up, the Mole was fishing. He had not had a bite all day, but he was perfectly happy dreaming in the sun, humming a little song.

Then he felt something on the end of his line.

He tugged hard. "This *is* a big one," he thought. "Yippee!"

He tugged harder. "This must be enormous," he thought. "Hooray!"

He gave an extra big tug. "This must be a whale!" he thought. "My goodness!"

He said "My goodness!" because at that moment he fell back in the boat as his line came up with something on the end of it. It was the glass slipper.

It was all covered with green stuff and Moley didn't know what to make of it. He put it in the boat and rowed to the bank and then took it into his little home in the river bank.

He took off the green stuff and saw by the dazzle that it was a glass slipper.

But what use is a glass slipper?

Moley couldn't wear it because his paws were too tiny.

He couldn't dig with it, because it might break.

He couldn't use it as a fruit bowl because it was the wrong shape.

Moley sat and looked at the glass slipper and didn't know what to do.

And that is where it is to this day. It's very much admired by his friends, who really don't know what he ought to do with it.

It stands on his mantelpiece, gleaming and glittering. But it doesn't *do* very much.

After all its story was over when the story of Cinderella ended so happily.

Perhaps, one day Moley will throw it back into the river and make a wish.

I think that's the best way, don't you?

19

Mickey Takes The Air

YOU ALL KNOW that Mickey Mouse was once apprentice to a Sorcerer—a powerful magician, who could make the wind and the sea dance to his bidding.

Well, Mickey had lots of adventures with the Sorcerer. Most of the adventures came when Mickey tried to do spells himself and got them wrong.

This is one of them.

One day Mickey was stirring some foul-smelling liquid, containing toad-slime and cockroach eggs, for his master when he heard the Sorcerer talking.

He was talking to his friend the Witch, who wasn't a very unpleasant witch. She just looked ugly, with a warty nose and cross eyes.

Now Mickey knew that the Witch had a flying broom-stick. And it was something that he had always wanted to try out.

"She's bound to be talking for a long time," he thought to himself. "I'll find out where it's parked and try it out for myself."

He sneaked out of the cave and there was the broom-stick, waiting for the

Witch, stood up against the cave entrance.

Mickey sat astride it.

"Go boy!" he called.

Nothing happened...

"Heigh ho, Silver!" he shouted.

Nothing happened.

Unknown to Mickey, the Sorcerer and the Witch were peering out at the strange noise from a window in the cave and laughing quietly to themselves at Mickey's naughtiness.

Then the Sorcerer nudged the Witch and the Witch muttered a spell under her breath:

"Oh, magic broom-stick fly for me!

And give our Mickey lots to see!"

Mickey was still shouting at the broom-stick.

And suddenly he was airborne.

Mickey grabbed hold of the stick as he saw the ground dwindle away from him. He was climbing so fast a lazy seagull stood stock still in mid-air, gaping at him in astonishment.

"Slow down," called Mickey.

The broom-stick kept on going faster.

Suddenly a jet plane zoomed past them. The pilot rubbed his eyes and said: "I don't believe it. It's not really happening."

But it was happening all right for Mickey.

"Oh dear, I never knew I didn't like heights," he said as the broom-stick went higher and higher.

Clouds whistled past. Now, Mickey could hardly see the ground; it was so far away it looked like a postage stamp.

"I'll never play tricks again," said Mickey.

Then, suddenly, the broom-stick stood upright, just like a bucking bronco trying to get rid of its rider.

It got rid of Mickey all right. He started to fall. The sky dizzied around his eyes. The ground whirled around under him. He was going faster . . . and faster.

And then he woke up. Was it only a dream?

As he blinked his eyes he saw the Sorcerer and the Witch standing above him. Both were laughing.

"Get on with your work," said the Sorcerer. Then he added as they walked to the door of the cave: "And stop sky-dreaming!"

The Tale of a Siamese

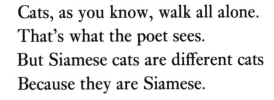

Cats, as you know, walk all alone.
That's what the poet sees.
But Siamese cats are different cats
Because they are Siamese.

They are elegant cats,
They are yowl-y cats,
And their cry is a cry forlorn.
They will cry so loud, they will cry so long,
It sounds like a babe, new-born.

Do you want to know why their yell is fierce?
Why their cry hits top-notes true?
It's because you see, being Siamese
They want to be with you.

For cats, as you know, walk all alone.
But everyone agrees
That Siamese cats are different cats
Because they are Siamese.

Donald Duck's Busy Day

YOU ALL KNOW DONALD DUCK, don't you? Of course! He is one of your favourite characters.

Sometimes he is rather grumpy. Sometimes he loses his temper and flies into a terrible rage. Sometimes he does some rather silly things. However, he has two great qualities: his goodheartedness and his unselfishness. These make one forget all his failings.

Donald lives with his three nephews, Huey, Dewey and Louie. Sometimes they are very naughty and their mischievous tricks make Donald very angry. Can you see them in the picture making a mess on the floor that Donald has just cleaned? But Donald is very good to them and looks after them very well.

In fact, Donald has a very busy life. He gets up very early and cleans the whole house. His little nephews often get in his way and make his work much harder. When he has given his little nephews breakfast, he sends them off to school. Then he goes to work himself.

When he comes home in the afternoon he makes a lovely tea. Then his little nephews come running in. They are usually very hungry and eat up all the cakes and jellies that Donald has made.

Then Donald plays a jolly game with them before he puts them to bed. How quiet and peaceful the house is then! Huey, Dewey and Louie get up very early and then Donald's busy day begins all over again.

The Three Little Pigs

ONCE UPON A TIME, there were three little pigs. They were very happy little pigs and often played jolly music together, but they didn't like the wicked old wolf.

One day they each decided to build a little house, so that the wolf couldn't catch them.

The little pig who played the flute was very lazy. He made his house of sticks and straw and it was soon finished. Then the wicked wolf came along. He huffed and he puffed and he blew the house down!

The little pig who played the violin made his house of wood. But the wicked wolf blew it down quite easily. Just two puffs and the house came crashing down.

Now the third little pig who played the piano was very sensible. *He* made his house of bricks and cement. It took him a long time but when it was finished it was a very strong little house. Soon the wicked wolf came along. He saw the house and cried, "I'll soon have that house down!" He huffed and he puffed, and he puffed and he huffed, but the house just didn't move. The poor wolf had to slink miserably away.

The hard-working little pig was very pleased. He sat down at his piano and played this merry tune, singing at the top of his voice:

"Who's afraid of the Big Bad Wolf,
The Big Bad Wolf, the Big Bad Wolf?
Who's afraid of the Big Bad Wolf?"
How cross the wolf was when he heard it!

23

Mickey Takes Photos

ONE DAY, the editor of the newspaper where Mickey worked ordered him to take some photographs for an article in the newspaper on "The Life of the Crocodile."

So Mickey packed his suitcase and his big camera and flew off in an aeroplane to Africa.

When he arrived, he marched through the jungle until he came to a huge river.

"I am sure there are many crocodiles in this river," said Mickey to himself. "I'll look for a good place to set up my camera."

Just then he saw the wide trunk of a tree floating in the water. Carefully he jumped on to it. But to his great astonishment he found that it wasn't a tree-trunk but a sleeping crocodile!

Poor Mickey had a terrible shock. Quickly he lifted his camera and jumped on to the shore.

The crocodile was very angry. He opened his mouth wide and showed his long sharp teeth.

Mickey took one look at him and said to himself, "I don't feel much like photographing crocodiles today," and lifting his camera on to his shoulder he hurried away from the river as fast as he could.

He really had quite a lucky escape, didn't he?

24

Goofy's Bicycle

EVERY DAY, when he went to work, Goofy stared with envy at all those people who were riding their bicycles, while he had to travel in the crowded tram.

"How I hate being pushed and shoved like this," he said to himself. "I wish *I* had a bicycle. But they are so expensive."

"Why don't you buy a second-hand one?" said one of his friends.

It seemed a very good idea. The trouble was he only had a little money, and so he had to buy a very, very old bicycle. You should have seen it! It was the sort of bicycle called a Penny-Farthing, with a huge wheel in the front and a little wheel at the back. How everyone laughed when they saw him wobbling by!

But Goofy didn't care. He was perfectly happy. "It suits me fine," he said. "I know it's not very modern, but riding this is much better than being in that stuffy old tram."

Indeed Goofy got lots of fun out of his old bicycle. He practised every day and he soon learned to ride it well. Soon he was able to ride to work. *And* he got to work on time!

Look at him in the picture.

He really does seem to be enjoying himself, doesn't he?

Uncle Scrooge's Good Turn

UNCLE SCROOGE is the richest duck in all the world. He lives in a huge house and he is so afraid of burglars that he has strong iron bars on all the windows, so that they cannot break in.

But sad to say there's something about him that is not very nice—although he is so rich, Uncle Scrooge is very, very mean. He spends all the day counting his money and his favourite music is the tinkle the coins make as they strike against each other. He hates to spend any of his money and keeps it in a big steel box.

One day, a poor little boy in the street asked him for a penny, but Uncle Scrooge wouldn't give him one. That night, when Uncle Scrooge went to bed, he just couldn't get to sleep. He realised that he

had behaved very badly. All night long he tossed and turned, and when morning came he was still awake.

There was only one thing to do.

He got out of bed, took out his steel box and counted out a big pile of money. Then he dressed quickly and, holding the money in his hat, went into the town to the Children's Hospital. He gave all the money to the matron of the hospital as a gift for the children.

That night he slept very well indeed. In fact, it was the best night's sleep he had ever had. Uncle Scrooge decided that in future he would try to stop being so mean, for the only way to be really happy was to be kind and unselfish.

And that's true, isn't it?

Pluto Digs a Hole

DO YOU KNOW what Pluto loves more than anything in the world? A good, juicy bone.

When he didn't feel hungry, he used to hide his bone so that he could eat it another day. He would find a safe spot and dig a big hole and put the bone in it, and then cover it up with earth. When he felt hungry again, he used to go and dig it up.

Well, one day Pluto was playing on the beach with his bone. Then he decided to go and have a little paddle in the sea. First he had to hide his bone. So, as he usually did, he dug a hole in the sand.

To his great surprise, he felt a sharp nip on his black nose. A little crab, angry at being disturbed, had caught it tightly in his claws!

"What do you think you're doing?" asked the crab crossly. "Don't you know this is my home?"

Pluto fell back on the sand yelping with pain. Then, barking loudly, he dashed off across the sand, forgetting all about his beautiful bone. "Whoof! Whoof!"

Now Pluto is very careful when he chooses a spot to bury a bone. He doesn't want to meet another little crab!

The Ugly Duckling

ONCE UPON A TIME, there was a little duckling who was very unhappy. None of the other ducklings loved him—because he was very ugly. The poor little one felt very sad and lonely because no one played with him. One day he decided to leave the pond where he lived. He couldn't stand the jeers of his companions any longer!

"I'll go and look for adventure," he said to himself. "I'm sick of being laughed at."

As he waddled along, he thought sadly of his misfortune.

"It's not my fault," he said, "that I am so ugly. Why wasn't I born beautiful like the other ducklings? Quack! Quack!"

But one day he had the greatest surprise of his life! He was feeling rather thirsty so he went towards the river in order to have a drink. He bent his head down to the water . . . Oh, wonderful! The figure he saw reflected in the water was that of a beautiful swan! He could hardly believe his eyes!

A new world opened at his feet. He was no longer an ugly duckling!

Gracefully, he swam on the river back to his home. Everyone looked at him.

"What a beautiful swan!" they cried. "You must stay with us."

So he did. How happy he was at last.

Minnie's Lovely Flowers

IN SPRINGTIME, Minnie's garden is a wonderful sight. The beds of flowers are beautifully tidy, the hedges neatly cut, and the grass is smooth as a carpet. The roses, carnations, sweet peas and tulips have a warmth and colour which has rarely been seen, and their scent is delightful.

Of course, Minnie works very hard keeping the garden like this, but when she sees it looking so beautiful she feels that all her hard work has been worthwhile.

"Perhaps I'll win first prize in the Flower Show next week!" she said to herself one day.

That evening there was a ring at her front door. It was Mickey who had come to call on her. "These are for you," he said, presenting her with a huge bunch of flowers.

"Oh, how lovely!" cried Minnie. As she lifted them up to smell them, she thought they looked rather familiar.

"Where did you get these beautiful flowers from?" she asked Mickey.

Mickey smiled. "From your garden," he said. "I wanted to give you the very best flowers, but, you know, they are very expensive so I . . ."

Mickey stopped in astonishment. Minnie had fainted!

Thumper's Advice

BAMBI LIKES GOING OUT for a walk with his friend Thumper Rabbit because his friend explains many things to him. The little rabbit is older than Bambi. He has lived in the wood a long time and he knows much more about the world than the little fawn.

Thumper Rabbit tells Bambi all kinds of things—the names of all the different butterflies and flowers, what kind of grass he should eat, where he should shelter when it rains, where he should sleep, what to do if danger should come. Bambi always listens very carefully, and tries to remember the clever advice of his friend.

For Bambi is very sensible. He knows that he must learn many things before he can become a good and wise leader, the Prince of the Forest.

And although he is still very young, Bambi knows the most important thing of all: that he knows very little.

"One day you will know many things," said Thumper Rabbit to Bambi, "then everyone will call you ' Wise One'."

Thumper Rabbit was right, wasn't he ?

For when Bambi grew up he *did* become the Prince of the Forest.

Professor Bookworm

PROFESSOR LUDWIG VON DRAKE, known to everyone by his nickname—Professor Bookworm—is the wisest duck in the world. He knows absolutely *everything*. He lives in a house full of books and is always studying one with the greatest attention. That's why he's called Professor Bookworm.

Can you see him in the picture studying his book?

He looks very wise, doesn't he?

He appears on the television often, in conferences and discussions of every kind. (Have you ever seen him?) He is able to talk about anything from traffic problems to flights in space. In fact, there isn't a single thing he *doesn't* know.

In order to know as much as this you must study and work very hard. It's for this reason that wise people are respected by all.

Wouldn't you like to grow up to be very wise?

You will have to do a lot of reading!

Panchito the Cockerel

"HALLO, LITTLE FRIENDS! How are things?

"I'm Panchito, the bravest cockerel in all Mexico. I was born in Jalisco, the best-known town in the whole country.

"I'm a great friend of Donald Duck of North America, and of Pedro the Parrot from Brazil. The three of us are known all over the world as 'The Three Caballeros'. Sometimes we get together and then we have a wonderful time.

"Right now I am on my way to fetch them. It's time we had a new adventure.

Together we will play our guitars and sing this beautiful song:

'We are the three Caballeros
One for all
And all for o-o-o-one!'
Do you know this song? Well, you can sing it with us! Ready?
'The three Caballeros!
The three Caballeros!
One for all
And all for o-o-o-one!
We are the three Caballeros!' "

The Lesson of Cinderella

WHEN POOR CINDERELLA, who was left all alone in the world, had to work as a simple servant, at the beck and call of her cruel stepsisters and stepmother, she didn't for a moment lose her good nature and high spirits.

She had to work very, very hard. She got up early every morning before the sun had risen over the hills and worked until long after the sun had set. All day long she did one job after another—sweeping, scrubbing, washing the clothes and the dishes, while her selfish sisters passed the day trying to make themselves beautiful. This was an impossible task for they were both very ugly and it only made them bad-tempered. They quar-relled with each other and they scolded Cinderella unmercifully.

But Cinderella never said an angry word. She worked merrily, singing a gay little song, for she knew that she was doing every job as well as she could and that made her happy.

As everyone knows, Cinderella got her reward at last. It was *she* who married the handsome prince and went to live in the beautiful castle. However, the lesson that Cinderella teaches us is that we must do our work well, however humble and difficult it may be, without losing our high spirits.

If we're happy and gay, we always get the work done quicker, don't we?

The Fierce Wolf

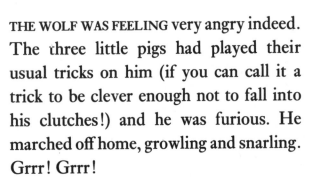

THE WOLF WAS FEELING very angry indeed. The three little pigs had played their usual tricks on him (if you can call it a trick to be clever enough not to fall into his clutches!) and he was furious. He marched off home, growling and snarling. Grrr! Grrr!

When he arrived at his house, he kicked the door open, then went in, slamming the door loudly behind him. He really was in a terrible temper . . .

The little wolf-cub who was having his supper looked up in surprise. "What's the matter, papa?" he asked, looking at the wolf's angry face.

"Grrr!" growled the wolf. "It's those miserable friends of yours. I tried to catch them and ran after them, but they had dug a large hole in the ground and I fell inside. I hit my head hard and almost broke it in two. And yet, *you*, my son, play with them and call them your friends."

The little wolf cub looked at his father.

"Papa," said the little wolf sweetly, "would you have fallen if you hadn't been chasing them?"

The fierce wolf growled, but he didn't say a word. There are some questions it's better not to answer.

Lady and The Tramp

LADY WAS A PRETTY little dog who lived happily with her master and mistress, Jim Dear and Darling.

She had two very good friends who lived in the same road. They were two marvellous dogs called Jock and Trusty and the three of them played happily together every day.

One day, Aunt Sara came to stay with Jim Dear and Darling. Now Aunt Sara had two wicked cats called Si and Am. They treated Lady so badly and made her life so miserable that one day she decided to run away . . .

Lady met a mongrel dog called Tramp. Although he was rough, he was a very kind dog and he and Lady had many exciting adventures together.

One night a huge rat crept into the nursery where the baby was sleeping. Tramp saw him. At once he rushed after him and, after a terrible fight, Tramp killed the rat.

Aunt Sara heard the noise and, not knowing what had really happened, she locked up Tramp. The next day she asked the Dog-Catcher to take him away. The Dog-Catcher put Tramp into his van but just as he was starting Jock and Trusty managed to jump on it and undo the catch. At once Tramp jumped out. He was free again!

Meanwhile, Aunt Sara found the dead rat lying behind the curtain. At once she realised that it was Tramp who had saved the baby from grave danger.

Now Tramp lives in the house with Lady and they are both very happy.

The Sorcerer's Apprentice

ONE DAY, while the Sorcerer was sleeping, Mickey, who was his apprentice, opened the huge book in which were written the magic spells. Mickey was feeling rather lazy and he wanted to find a spell which would help him to get water from the well.

Mickey found just the spell he wanted. So he chanted it over a broom that was standing in a corner. At once the broom picked up a bucket and marched off to the well. A few moments later it was back, carrying the bucket full of water. Soon Mickey had enough water but he didn't know the spell to make the broom stop!

The broom went on marching down to the well and back again with more and more water, until the whole house was flooded!

Mickey didn't know what to do. He screamed and yelled at the broom, but it just would not stop. The water got higher and higher . . .

Just then the Sorcerer woke up. He gave a terrible cry when he saw all the water, and then quickly said the magic words. The broom stopped at once.

The Sorcerer was very angry. He gave Mickey a good scolding for doing such a silly thing.

Mickey realised then that to be a good sorcerer you must know how to make spells stop, too. It would be a long time before *he* would be a real sorcerer.

The Adventure of Little Tramp

LITTLE TRAMP, the puppy, was always dreaming of being as brave and strong as his father, Tramp, the mongrel dog. Little Tramp was very proud of his father, for he had had so many exciting adventures.

One day, Little Tramp ran away from the house. He was determined to find a dangerous adventure somewhere. Soon he saw a milkman's cart and he chased it, barking loudly in order to show how brave he was. Wouff! Wouff!

Following the milkman's cart he entered the garden of a house where many children lived. To his great surprise, as soon as they saw him they jumped on him and put him in a cage!

Little Tramp looked around in astonishment. There were lots of animals in cages—rabbits, guinea-pigs, tortoises, mice. You see, these children were very fond of animals and so they had made a little zoo of their very own.

But Little Tramp didn't like being locked up in a cage. He whimpered and cried and barked so much that the children's mother came out into the garden.

"You naughty children! You can't lock up a little puppy like this," she said, as soon as she saw Little Tramp. And she set the puppy free.

Little Tramp gave a little bark of joy and wagged his tail happily. Then he ran home as quickly as he could.

He'd had enough of adventures for the time being. He promised himself that he wouldn't look for more until he was grown-up.

Brer Rabbit Plays with Tar

BRER BEAR AND BRER FOX were very angry. Brer Rabbit had played so many tricks on them that they were longing to teach him a lesson.

One day they had a good idea. They made a puppet out of tar and then they put a jacket on it, and a hat on its head. It looked quite real. Then they put the puppet by the side of the road.

After a while, Brer Rabbit came along, whistling merrily. He saw the puppet and, thinking it was a traveller who was resting, he said, "Good morning," politely.

But the traveller didn't answer. "Good morning," said Brer Rabbit again, in a louder voice. Still no reply. Brer Rabbit was very angry by now so he gave the traveller a rap on the nose. The tar had melted in the hot sun and so Brer Rabbit's paw stuck to the puppet. He pulled and pulled, but he couldn't get away! Just then Brer Bear and Brer Fox, who had been hiding in the bushes, came out and took Brer Rabbit prisoner.

"Please don't hurt me, fellows," cried Brer Rabbit. "I promise I won't play any more tricks on you."

Brer Bear and Brer Fox looked at Brer Rabbit and then at each other and laughed. Brer Rabbit was covered in tar by now and looked a terrible mess. So they let him go.

Brer Rabbit had learned his lesson and he didn't play any more tricks on them. At least—not for a long time!

No Customers for The Mad Hatter

THE MAD HATTER sat glumly in his little shop and sighed:

"Dearie me!"

He sighed again:

"Oh, lack-a-day!"

And again:

"It's so sad!"

Why was the Mad Hatter so unhappy? No customers. Nobody had come into his shop all day. He had not sold a single hat.

"I shall have to shut up shop," he said to himself.

Then there came a fierce knocking at the shop-door.

The Mad Hatter hurried to open it.

There were his friends, the March Hare and The Dormouse.

"Where were you?" they asked.

"Inside my shop, waiting for customers. But I haven't had any customers," said the Mad Hatter.

"No wonder," said the March Hare.

"No wonder," squeaked the Dormouse.

On the shop door was the sign saying "CLOSED". The Mad Hatter had forgotten to turn it round to read "OPEN".

"You really are crazy," said the March Hare.

"Crazy," echoed the Dormouse.

And the Mad Hatter laughed and said: "How true!"

Mice on The Moon

IT WAS THE DAY of The Rocket.

Everybody, but everybody, was gathered at Cape Kennedy to watch the mighty rocket streak off to the moon. If they were not at Cape Kennedy they were watching the excitement on television or hearing about it on the radio.

Such excitement!

So much excitement that nobody noticed two small, plump mice who were making themselves very much at home on the rocket-site.

Jaq, the chief cheesetaster at Cinderella's Palace, and his friend, Gus, had travelled all the way just to see what the excitement was all about.

And when they saw the rocket they knew. It stood above them like a great black needle about to stitch up the sky. Clouds of smoke cushioned it on the launching pad.

Gus blew a few bubbles nervously from his bubble-pipe.

Jaq said pompously: "Stop playing with that silly toy, Gus! Here is Man's greatest achievement—and all you can do is play at blowing bubbles."

Gus said: "How does it work, Jaq?"

Jaq said: "Er . . . er . . . I know we'll go inside the rocket and I'll give you a lesson in elementary physics."

"Yes please," sighed Gus.

The two little mice threaded their way through the forest of human legs that was the crowd at the rocket site, went through several doors marked "Do Not Enter" and "Visitors Not Allowed," and ended up in a room that had two portholes and a lot of levers and switches.

"I don't think we should be here," said Gus, nervously.

"Nonsense, mon ami," said Jaq. "It's all quite straightforward. The fuel is injected via pipes down there during the countdown and then—"

And then? SOMETHING happened.

You've guessed it. There was a shudder like a giant makes when he wakes up, there was a noise like a million electric kettles boiling over and Gus and Jaq both gave little squeaks of terror:

"Eeeek!"

Gus had pulled the wrong lever.

The rocket had started to fly. Heading for the moon. Gus and Jaq rushed to one of the portholes and peered out. Already the earth was the size of a baseball in the distance, and it was getting smaller.

"What *are* we going to do?" squeaked Gus. "We have no space helmets. How are we going to breathe?"

Now Jaq may sometimes be pompous, but he can be very quick-thinking.

"Your bubble pipe," he said.

Gus soon got the idea. He blew two enormous bubbles and they fitted them over their heads just like space helmets. Their voices were a bit muffled, but they were all right behind the transparent pane of bubble.

"Now all we have to do is wait," said Jaq. "Thanks to me we'll be all right."

Gus said: "Thanks to me—and my silly bubble-pipe."

"Don't let's argue," said Jaq.

Then they sat down very close to each other.

Outside they could hear the whistle of the rocket-engine. They could see the pinpricks of light that were stars. Nearer than they had ever seen them before.

Ahead of them the moon peered up at them, its face getting bigger and bigger.

Gus and Jaq sat and waited for the bump.

They felt a little cold and perhaps a little scared. But they didn't say anything to each other.

Then the bump happened.

It was a very gentle bump. It hardly shook them at all.

They stood looking through the port-hole at the strange landscape around them. Everything looked silver and cold, because there was no light at that time to give it all colour.

"Wwwhat shall we do?" quavered Gus.

"Follow me," commanded Jaq. "This is a great adventure. We will be the first mice to set foot on the moon!"

"Shouldn't you have a flag to plant on the moon's surface?" asked Gus.

Gus took out a handkerchief. It was a bit grubby but upon it he drew the emblem of Cinderella's kingdom which was a pumpkin. They opened the cabin door—and stepped out on to the moon.

It smelled very strange.

Undaunted, the mice stepped forward and Gus made a little speech about claiming the moon for Cinderella and her Prince. Then they planted the flag in the moon's surface.

"Now what do we do?" said Gus, miserably.

"What do you want to do?" said Jaq.

"Eat," said Gus promptly. "I'm starving!"

They turned out their pockets, but there was nothing there to eat. There was a cat-whistle, some cat-nip and a catapault. But nothing to eat.

Gus rubbed his round tummy and moaned:

"Oh, dear I'm so hungry."

"Don't worry, old chum," said Jaq, putting his paw around his little friend's shoulders. "It'll all be all right."

"Will it?" squeaked Gus.

"Of course," said Jaq. "Just wait until the sun comes up, then you'll feel warmer."

"It's the earth that rises here," said Gus.

"I won't argue," said Jaq.

At that moment, earth dawned.

Its light flooded across the moon and the two mice felt warmer as they saw colour spread across the moonscape.

And they saw what colour it was. Green.

"I don't believe it," said Jaq.

"What?" said Gus.

Jaq broke off a piece of the moon and sniffed it and then—ate it.

"It's true," he shouted. "It's true. The moon is made of green cheese."

It was true.

Both mice started tucking in to a hearty meal until, fat and full, they were both satisfied. Then they sat back, happily.

"Jaq," said Gus sleepily.

"Yes," said Jaq.

"Do you think we'll ever be rescued?"

"Of course we will," said Jaq.

But he was not really so sure. And he didn't really care. Not with all that green cheese around them.

"I never thought I'd say it," said Jaq, a little while later.

"What?" said Gus.

"I'm fed up with cheese," said Jaq despondently.

They seemed to have been there on the moon for ages. And cheese was everywhere. Both little mice smelled of cheese. The trouble was that there was no variety.

No Stilton, no Gorgonzola, no Cheddar, no Cheshire. Just green cheese.

The two mice sat looking miserable.

Then they heard the noise.

It was a rocket from earth.

Jaq and Gus cheered like mad. They ran to and fro trying to attract the attention of the astronauts.

Suddenly, Gus stopped: "I say . . ." he said.

"What?" said Jaq.

"Perhaps those astronauts will be angry with us for taking one of their rockets."

"I hadn't thought of that," said Jaq.

"Oh, dear," they both said.

With a great belch of fire and a huge mountain of smoke the rocket landed. Two astronauts got out.

The two mice hid behind a green cheese boulder and listened.

One astronaut was telling the other about the green cheese.

The other was discovering the rocket that had brought the two mice to the moon.

Neither of them knew that it was Jaq and Gus who had come on the rocket.

"Quick!" shouted Jaq.

While the two astronauts weren't looking the two mice dashed on board the rocket and lay quivering underneath a bunk.

They heard the astronauts claim the moon on behalf of earth. They heard them talking to the folk back home on earth. Then the two astronauts got into the rocket—and took off.

It seemed to take longer to get back to earth than it had done to get to the moon.

But they *did* arrive back at Cape Kennedy.

And in all the bustle and confusion of congratulations who would notice two small mice, climbing out of the rocket and heading back home?

Nobody.

Of course, when they saw the newspapers next day and saw that the astronauts were getting the credit for being the first on the moon Jaq and Gus were a little peeved.

After all *they* had been first on the moon.

But they didn't worry for long. They were too busy eating.

But it wasn't cheese they were stuffing beneath their whiskers.

It was bacon rind.

Morning Newspaper

PONGO, the father of all those dalmations, got a pat on the head from his master and his instructions: "Now, Pongo, old boy the newspaper lad hasn't called this morning. So I'd like you to go along to the newsagents and pick up the morning paper. I'll phone and let him know that you're coming."

So Pongo, head held high, trotted out into the early morning street, very conscious of what an important job he had to do. He knew that his master liked to read the paper at breakfast—even though his mistress didn't care for it.

Pongo sniffed at the air. He smelled that a strange dog had walked down the street that morning. "I wonder who he is and what he wants," thought Pongo.

Further on he saw a golden cocker spaniel—the stranger.

"Good morning," said the stranger. "I'm visiting friends round here."

"Good morning," said Pongo. "Hope that you enjoy your stay."

Pongo sniffed at the air again and this time smelled that a tom cat he knew was nearby. "I wonder if I ought to chase him just for a bit of fun," thought Pongo.

Then he saw the cat, who was smiling. "I'm so happy," said the cat, "I've just become the father of five of the most beautiful kittens in the world. Aren't I lucky, Pongo?"

"Congratulations," said Pongo, deciding that it wouldn't be fair to chase the cat when he was so happy. "It's

great being a father. I know only too well."

Nose still well up in the air, Pongo trotted towards the newsagents. This time he smelled that cheeky squirrel, who always forgot where he hoarded his nuts. "He's up and about early," thought Pongo.

Then he reached the newsagents. The newsagent was there with Pongo's paper ready for him. "There's a good, clever boy," said the newsagent.

"Anybody would think there was something unusual about fetching a newspaper," thought Pongo, as he started back again for home. He sniffed the air again.

He could smell that another cat had been along here before him.

He could smell that the milk-van had been out and about.

He could smell the petrol fumes from the cars that had been travelling along the road.

Then he could smell . . . breakfast!

Pongo ran a little now. He had not realised how hungry he was.

Pongo's master met him at the door. "Good dog, Pongo," he said, taking the newspaper from Pongo's mouth. "Your breakfast is ready."

Pongo started to eat the meat in his bowl as his master sat down to look at the paper.

"Now I'll be able to read the news," he said.

"Funny," thought Pongo, "I've *smelled* all the news of the morning. That walk was my morning newspaper."

Roquefort Meets a Strange Little Mouse

ONE MORNING the three little kittens, Marie, Berlioz and Toulouse, knocked at the door of Roquefort's mousehole. Roquefort the mouse was their friend and they had brought him a surprise.

The door opened and Roquefort's little head popped out. "What is it?" he squeaked.

"Look!" mewed the little kittens excitedly. "Here's a new friend for you."

Roquefort stared. There stood a strange little mouse. A brown furry mouse with a long, long tail. Roquefort sniffed and twitched his little whiskers. "Who is he?" he squeaked.

"His name is Camembert," said Marie. "He's come to live with you. He'll cheer you up and stop you feeling lonely."

Roquefort sniffed. He didn't need cheering up and he didn't feel at all lonely, but he didn't want to hurt the little kittens because he knew they were only being kind.

"Oh, thank you very much," he said, looking very suspiciously at the stranger.

"Well, take him into your house, Roquefort," said Berlioz. "I expect he'd like some breakfast. We'll see you later,"

and off the little kittens scampered.

Roquefort stared at the brown mouse. He was a very quiet mouse. In fact, he didn't give a single squeak. "Well, you'd better come in," said Roquefort, and he pushed open the door of his mousehole.

But the strange little mouse didn't move.

"Come on, don't be shy!" said Roquefort, and he gave him a gentle push.

What a funny walk the stranger had! He sort of slid over the floor instead of walking like a *normal* little mouse.

"I expect you're quite hungry," said Roquefort, politely, to his visitor.

But the little brown mouse didn't say a word.

Roqefort took out his very best cheese from the larder and his delicious fruit-cake which he kept for special occasions. He put some in front of Camembert. "There, old chap," he said. "Don't be shy. Eat away!"

But the little stranger only stared. He wouldn't eat a thing!

"Oh, dear," thought Roquefort. "What am I going to do with him?" Then, politely, he tried to make conversation. "Are you from these parts? You'll like this house. Duchess and her three kittens are most unusual cats. *True* aristocats. And very friendly. We have lots of happy times. And such good food, for Madame Bonfamille is a *real* lady. . ."

But the little brown mouse didn't say a word. Not even one tiny squeak. Roquefort felt very miserable. What was he going to do?

Suddenly there was a tiny tap at his door. Roquefort opened it. There stood the three kittens. "How is your new friend, Roquefort?" they asked.

Roquefort twitched his whiskers. "I don't know what to do with him," he said. "He won't eat, and he won't talk, and he won't move."

"*You* wouldn't either if you were a TOY MOUSE!" said Marie. And the three kittens laughed so much that they rolled over.

"A TOY MOUSE!" cried Roquefort, in surprise.

"Yes, you didn't think we'd want another *real* mouse in this house, did you?" said Berlioz.

Roquefort breathed a sigh of relief.

"You're the nicest mouse in the whole world, Roquefort," said Toulouse.

"We couldn't share you with *anyone*," said the three cheeky little kittens all at the same time.

Roquefort twitched his sharp little nose. Then softly he breathed a great big sigh of relief.

Brer Fox and The Caterpillar

ONE DAY BRER FOX was creeping through the fields when he saw a caterpillar sliding through the grass.

"Hullo, you funny little thing!"

"I'm not a funny little thing!" said the caterpillar indignantly. "I bet I can run faster than you."

"Faster than *me*!" said Brer Fox in surprise, and he laughed so much that his sides ached.

"I'll start behind you," said the caterpillar, "and even then I'll reach the stream before you!"

Brer Fox couldn't understand this at all. How could such a funny little creature run faster than he could? "I'll show him," he said to himself.

So he stood in front of the caterpillar and the clever little caterpillar climbed up Brer Fox's tail and clung to the tip. Then he cried out, "Are you ready? One, two, three—go!"

Off flew Brer Fox as fast as the wind. He soon reached the bank of the stream. He turned round to see if the caterpillar was coming. As he swung his tail the little caterpillar was flicked into the air and he flew over to the other side of the stream.

"Where are you, slowcoach?" shouted Brer Fox.

"I'm here," said a little voice from the far bank. "I've been waiting for ages. I was tired of waiting for you, so I just swam across the stream."

Brer Fox was so angry that he tucked his tail between his legs and slunk away without saying another word.

Mowgli Tricks The Monkey King

SOMETIMES MOWGLI had to go to school in the village with the other children. He hated this and instead of doing his sums like a good boy he used to look out of the window at the jungle. His friends were there and he longed to play with them.

One day Mowgli was very naughty. "I won't go to school today," he said. "I'll go and see how my friends are getting on."

So off he wandered into the jungle. It was lovely and cool in the shade of the trees. He walked by the river and picked some bananas. He climbed some rocks where he had a good view. But there was no sign of his friends Bagheera, the Panther, or Baloo, the Bear.

Mowgli began to feel sleepy. It really was very hot. So he sat down in the shade of a paw-paw tree and fell asleep.

He awoke with a start. Something was crashing all around him! It was paw-paws. The big round fruit came tumbling down, CRASH! "Hey!" yelled Mowgli angrily. "What's going on?"

There was a great howling and shrieking and chattering. The tree was alive with monkeys! They flew from branch to branch catching each other's tails, making such a noise that poor Mowgli's head spun round and round.

Suddenly they caught hold of Mowgli and lifted him up.

"Stop it! Stop it!" yelled Mowgli angrily, kicking his dangling legs as the monkeys carried him high into the tree.

"The Monkey King wants to see you," chattered the monkeys. "Come on!" And

they swung Mowgli through the treetops.

Soon they reached the Ruined City deep in the jungle where the monkeys lived.

The Monkey King was waiting on his throne. "Hello, Man Cub," he grinned. "So nice of you to drop in and see us."

The monkeys dropped Mowgli to the ground in front of the throne. "What do you want?" said Mowgli angrily, picking himself up.

"Well, now," said the Monkey King, scratching his head. "We would just like to know one of your secrets. Man Cubs know so many secrets."

"Well, what is it?" said Mowgli im-

patiently. He hated the monkeys because they were so foolish, always playing silly tricks, always chattering without a stop, and unable to keep still for a moment.

"We want you to show us how to make mats so that we can have some shelter when it rains," said the Monkey King.

Mowgli groaned. It was impossible to teach the monkeys anything. They soon lost interest and began to fidget, and pull each other's tails and jump up and down on all fours.

"As soon as you've made up some nice mats you can go home," said the Monkey King slyly.

"But that's not fair," said Mowgli. "It

will take *ages*. And you monkeys never listen."

"But we will," said the Monkey King, jumping down from his throne. "Now, just tell us what you need."

Mowgli sighed. "Get me some thick, strong creepers."

Shrieking and chattering, the monkeys darted into the forest.

Soon they were back, trailing a thick clump of creepers behind them.

Mowgli picked up three of the creepers and began to work them in and out, making a thick, strong rope. "Now watch carefully," said Mowgli, "then you can try."

When Mowgli had finished the rope, he told the monkeys to start. "Get three creepers each," he said.

Shrieking with excitement, the monkeys dived at the mass of creepers, pulling and pushing each other out of the way. Now they started getting angry, biting and hitting each other. Soon the monkeys were a fighting, struggling heap all entangled in the creepers.

They were so busy that they didn't see what Mowgli was doing. Quick as a flash, he had thrown the thick rope in his hand around the Monkey King and tied it tight!

The Monkey King screamed and struggled but the monkeys were making so much noise that they did not hear him.

Quickly Mowgli darted away. He had to hurry. Those monkeys could run much faster than he could. Jumping over rocks, dodging between the old stone pillars, Mowgli raced away from the Ruined

City, hardly stopping to draw breath.

"Stop!" cried a familiar voice. It was Bagheera, the Panther.

"Oh, am I glad to see you!" cried the delighted Mowgli.

Mowgli jumped on Bagheera's back. Swiftly they rode through the jungle until they reached the village.

"Now be a good little Man Cub," said Bagheera. "You know you must go to school."

"Yes, you're right," sighed Mowgli. "The jungle is much too dangerous."

Winnie The Pooh Has A Sticky Problem

WINNIE-THE-POOH had a problem. It was Eeyore's birthday and he didn't know what to give him for a present. Should he give him a jar of honey, or a jar of condensed milk? Winnie-the-Pooh thought and thought, until his poor head was aching from thinking, but he just couldn't make up his mind. "I know," he suddenly said to himself. "I'll go and ask Owl. *He*'ll know what to do."

So off Winnie-the-Pooh went to the Hundred Acre Wood where Owl lived. He knocked at the knocker on the front door of "The Chestnuts" and waited.

At last the door opened. "Who is it?" said a rather cross voice. "I was having my little nap, you know. You creatures seem to forget that we owls stay awake all night. It's very tiring."

"It's only Me," said Winnie-the-Pooh, in a sorry sort of voice.

"Who is Me?" asked Owl, ruffling his feathers.

"*Me*. Winnie-the-Pooh," said Pooh Bear patiently.

"Ah! I see!" said Owl, opening one eye. "Well, what can I do for you?"

"Well, it's a very sticky question," said Winnie-the-Pooh. "It's the old grey donkey's birthday. Shall I give him a jar of honey or a jar of condensed milk?"

"That *is* sticky," said Owl, looking

very wise. "The question is—do donkeys like honey or do they like condensed milk?"

"I don't know," said Winnie-the-Pooh, "I *only* know what I like."

"And which one is that?" asked Owl.

"Both," said Winnie-the-Pooh, without any hesitation.

Owl blinked his eyes. "Ah, but if you *had* to choose, which one would you rather have?"

Winnie-the-Pooh thought and thought, and all the thinking about food made him long for a little something. "Oh, Owl, I don't know," said Pooh Bear sadly. "I'm too *hungry* to think."

"Ah! Ah!" said Owl, in a very pleased voice. "As you're so hungry, what do you

want to eat—honey or condensed milk?"

"Both," said Pooh, who was quite, quite sure.

There was a long, long silence. Owl was beginning to fall off to sleep and Winnie-the-Pooh was far-away, dreaming of honey or condensed milk. But then he remembered something . . .

"Owl," said Winnie-the-Pooh suddenly. "That's not the problem."

"No?" asked Owl in surprise.

"No," said Winnie-the-Pooh. "It's not what *I* prefer but it's what *Eeyore* would prefer."

"True. True," said Owl. "Oh, it *is* a difficult problem." He paused, scratched his head thoughtfully and then went on, "If there could only be honey *or* con-

densed milk in the world, which would be better?"

Winnie-the-Pooh looked horrified. "It's too terrible to *think* about it. How *could* you make such a suggestion, Owl?"

Owl looked very ashamed. Then suddenly he flapped his wings excitedly. "I've got it. Don't give him a jar of honey *or* a jar of condensed milk. Give him a jar of jam!"

Winnie-the-Pooh looked at Owl in astonishment. Slowly a great big grin spread over his face. "What a wonderful idea! What a simply wonderful idea! How *clever* you are, Owl!"

And off Pooh trotted to his house, feeling very pleased with himself. Thank goodness that sticky problem was solved!

Bambi Sees The Meadow

ONCE, WHEN BAMBI was very small, his mother said to him, "Soon we'll see the meadow."

"What's a meadow?" asked Bambi.

"You'll find out," said his mother. "Be a good little deer and be patient."

Bambi was *very* curious. He wondered and wondered what a meadow could be. Perhaps it was another animal. Perhaps it was a kind of tree.

One day Bambi was walking with his mother beneath the dark trees in the cool forest when he saw a strange patch of light ahead of him. The sky grew brighter and brighter, and the trees grew thinner and smaller.

Bambi wanted to bound forward into the bright yellow light because it looked so exciting. But his mother stopped him.

"What is it?" asked Bambi:

"It's the meadow," said his mother.

"Oh, let's go and see it," said Bambi impatiently.

"Wait," said his mother. "It's beautiful in the meadow, but dangerous, too. You must be very careful out there. If I call you, you must get behind me at once. I'll go first."

Bambi's mother walked out into the light, slowly and carefully. She lifted her head and listened and looked all around. Then she stretched herself, "Come, Bambi!" she called.

Bambi bounded out. In the forest he could only see little bits of blue through the tops of the trees, but now he could see the whole wide blue sky. In the forest he had sometimes seen a little sunbeam dancing here and there, but now he was standing in blinding hot sunlight. He shut his eyes and felt the wonderful warmth run right through him. He was

fanning its wings slowly. Then it spread its wings wide apart, till they were folded together like the sail of a ship, then raised them.

"Please sit still," Bambi said. "Just for a moment."

"Why should I sit still?" the insect said in astonishment.

"I want to see you close to. *Please*. You're so beautiful. Just like a flower!"

"What?" cried the butterfly, fanning his wings. "Did you say like a flower? We're much prettier than flowers!"

"Oh, yes," stammered Bambi, "*Much* prettier. I only meant . . ."

"Whatever you meant, it's all the same to me," said the butterfly, spreading his beautiful wings and twirling his delicate feelers. "Have you seen enough? I must be going." He moved his wings gently and gracefully. Then he fluttered off into the sunny air.

Bambi sighed with happiness. What a wonderful place the meadow was!

so happy he forgot to be worried.

He drank in the sweet fresh air and leaped into the air, three, four, *five* times. His mother came running up to him. "Catch me!" she called. And in a flash she was gone.

Bambi raced after her. He felt as if he were flying through the air. The swishing grass sounded wonderful. It felt as soft and fine as silk when it brushed against him.

When the race was over, Bambi looked all round him at the meadow. He was so surprised to see grass everywhere, and white daisies, purple clover blossoms and bright golden dandelion heads dotted all over it.

"Look, look, Mother!" exclaimed Bambi. "There's a flower flying!"

"That's not a flower," said his mother. "That's a butterfly."

Bambi stared in wonder at the butterfly. It fluttered about in a giddy sort of way and then stopped on a blade of grass,

Return Visit to Naboombu

DO YOU REMEMBER the story of Charlie, Carrie and Paul, the three orphans who went to stay with Miss Eglantine Price during the war? Well . . . one day Paul was playing with the Magic Bedknob which Miss Price, who was learning to be a witch, had given him.

"I wonder how our old friends in Naboombu are?" said Paul, rolling the Magic Bedknob in his hand.

"It would be lovely to see them again," said Carrie wistfully.

"I know what you're thinking," said a voice. It was Miss Price, who had just come into the room.

"Oh, do you think we could?" cried Paul, his eyes sparkling.

"Well . . ." said Miss Price doubtfully.

"Oh please!" said the three children all at once. "We haven't got anything to do today!"

"And it's so cold," said Charlie. "And

in Naboombu it will be so lovely and warm."

"Oh, all right!" said Miss Price. "But we mustn't be too long."

In great excitement they all piled on to the bed. Paul screwed the Magic Bedknob back on the bedpost and then tapped it. "Bed," he commanded, "take us to Naboombu!"

SWOOOOSH! The bed was up, off and over the sea. It flew through the sky, faster than an aeroplane, across England, far over the sea—on, on, on into another world . . .

Below them they could see the beautiful blue lagoon, and there was bear, still fishing!

"Why, hallo there!" he said. "We wondered when you'd be back. The King wants a word with you," he added rather sternly.

"Oh dear!" said Miss Price, remem-

bering that the last time she saw him she had turned him into a rabbit.

"Is he . . . is he . . ." she stammered.

"Oh, it's all right," said bear. "He's a lion again. But he had to stay a rabbit for six weeks and he didn't like that one little bit."

Miss Price looked anxiously at the children. "Perhaps we shouldn't bother the King just now," she said. "We'll come back another day."

"No, you'd better stay," said the bear. "He's got a problem, and it's making him very miserable."

"Perhaps we can help him," said Paul eagerly. "Let's go and see."

So the bear led them to the King.

It was all very quiet. In fact there wasn't a sound from the royal tent. They all followed the bear inside. The King was sitting on his throne, his head propped on his paw, looking very unhappy.

"Look who's here, your majesty," said the bear. "Some old friends of yours."

The King looked up, but there was no welcoming smile on his gloomy face. Then Miss Price was delighted to see that around his neck was hanging "The Star of Astooth".

"Oh, I'm so glad you got the Star back," said Miss Price. "It was mean of us to take it."

"Never mind about that," growled the King feebly. "Something much worse than that has happened."

"Oh dear!" said Paul. "What's wrong?"

The King looked at him with eyes full of sadness. A tear rolled out of the corner

of his eye and down his furry face.

"It's our football," he said in a voice of great sadness. "It's lost. Our very last one. Rhino gave it a magnificent header and it went far out to sea and disappeared. We haven't played for months."

"Oh, that's terrible!" said Miss Price. "What can we do?"

They all thought carefully. Suddenly Paul said what they were all thinking. "Couldn't you try some magic, Miss Price?"

Miss Price sighed. "Well, I've really given up being a witch," she said. "I haven't cast a spell for ages. I haven't even got my note-book with me. But I suppose I could try . . ."

"Oh, do!" cried the children. "It's awful to see the poor King so unhappy."

"All right," said Miss Price, very brisk and sensible. "Bring me twelve

coconuts, twelve of the biggest coconuts you can find."

Eagerly the children, followed by the bear, ran off into the jungle. Crocodile, Rhino and the other animals joined in the search.

Soon twelve beautiful coconuts were lined up on the football pitch outside the king's tent.

Miss Price stood in front of the coconuts and stared at them. Everyone was silent. The Lion King gazed intently at Miss Price.

Miss Price felt desperate. She was afraid she couldn't remember a single spell. She racked her brains to think a spell for changing things. "Football, football, football, football . . ." she whispered almost under her breath. Then she thought of all the names of football clubs she knew and whispered them like a great chant: Aston Villa, Manchester United, Derby County, Arsenal, Chelsea,

Fulham, Bristol Rovers, Crystal Palace, West Ham, Leeds, Wolves . . . Slowly she raised her arms, her voice became louder and louder. The famous names echoed around the football pitch.

Suddenly there was a great flash of light. The twelve coconuts went up in smoke! When the smoke had cleared away there lay twelve round beautiful leather footballs.

"Hurrah!" cried the king, throwing his crown into the air.

"Hurrah!" cried the children and all the animals.

"Thank goodness!" murmured Miss Price.

What a wonderful football match they had to celebrate.

Late that night, tired and dirty but very happy, they lay on the bed. Paul tapped the bedknob three times. Off they flew into the dark night sky. SWOOOSH! Soon they were safely home.

Pinocchio Meets a Sly Fox and a Wicked Cat

PINOCCHIO HAD BEEN SAVING UP his money to buy Geppetto a new overcoat. Now he had five pieces of gold.

One day as he was walking home he met a fox called J. Worthington Foulfellow, and a cat called Gideon. Pinocchio didn't know it, but they were really very wicked.

"Good morning, Pinocchio," said the fox. "I saw your father yesterday sitting on his doorstep without a coat. He was shivering with the cold."

"Well, he won't have to shiver any more," said Pinocchio. "I've got five pieces of gold and I'm going to buy him a new coat."

"I'll show you how to get twice as much money," said the cunning fox. "Come with us to Booby Land."

Now Pinocchio knew that he should go home, but Mr. Foulfellow and Mr. Gideon promised him so many wonderful things that he decided to go with them.

They walked quite a long way until it was dark. When they were out in the country in the middle of a lonely road, the fox suddenly caught hold of Pinocchio's arm. "Your money or your life!" he growled in a horrible voice.

Pinocchio was very frightened but, quick as a flash, he put his gold pieces into his mouth.

"Give us your money or we'll kill you!" screeched the cat.

"No. No. Never!" said Pinocchio, the money rattling in his mouth.

The fox realised at once what he had done. "Spit that money out!" he threatened.

"Give it here at once!" snarled the cat. And he put his paw between Pinocchio's lips, trying to force open his mouth.

Pinocchio bit his hand hard. "Yiaow!" yelled the cat. He was very, very angry.

"Let's tie him upside down on the

branch of a tree," said the fox. "When he opens his mouth the money will fall out."

So they tied Pinocchio to the tree. They waited and waited, but Pinocchio would not open his mouth.

"Oh, I'm tired of waiting," said the cat, whose paw was hurting. "Let's go to the inn and have a drink and then come back."

So off they went to the inn. Poor Pinocchio struggled and struggled but he couldn't undo the ropes.

Now, not far away, there was a little white house where the Blue Fairy lived. She knew that Pinocchio was in trouble. She went to the window and clapped her hands three times. At once a huge falcon flew to the window-sill.

"What can I do for you, kind fairy," the falcon asked bowing very low.

"Peck at the rope that is holding the puppet and put him at the foot of the tree," said the Blue Fairy.

So off the falcon flew and did as he was told.

Then the fairy called a magnificent spaniel who was dressed like a coachman. "Drive my coach to the tree and bring the puppet back," she said.

So the spaniel did.

Pinocchio soon felt better and told the Blue Fairy what had happened. "You're a good little puppet to save your money for Geppetto," said the Blue Fairy. "I'm sure that one day you will be a *real* boy. But you must watch out for that sly fox and the cat."

So Pinocchio did. He was always *very* careful in future.

Dumbo at the Fair

YOU ALL KNOW DUMBO, don't you? He's the little elephant with the big, big ears.

Well . . . one day Dumbo saw two children at the village fair. Dumbo watched them for a while. They were looking at the other children riding the roundabout and their faces were very sad.

"What's the matter?" asked Dumbo.

"We'd love to have a ride on the round-about," said the little girl.

"But we haven't any money," sighed the little boy.

"I've got a good idea," said Dumbo. "Why don't you come for a ride on me?"

The children clapped their hands with delight. "Oh, we'd love to!" they cried.

Eagerly, they climbed on to Dumbo's back. But to their great surprise, instead of walking, Dumbo FLEW!

Up . . . up . . . up they went. High into the air. Soon they were swooping over the village and the Fair was far below them. How small everyone looked!

"I didn't know elephants could FLY!" said the boy in wonder when they were back on the ground.

"Well, I'm rather a special sort of elephant," said Dumbo shyly.

"You're dear little Dumbo!" cried the girl, kissing him on the tip of his trunk. "How wonderful to meet you! And thank you so much for the lovely ride!"

The Wise Dwarf

ALL THE DWARFS who live with Snow-White in the little cottage in the middle of the wood always listen carefully to everything that Doc says. And they always do what he tells them.

And it's not just because he is the Chief of the Dwarfs. It's just that time has proved that he is the wisest one, the one who talks most sensibly and who always knows what is right and what is wrong. For Doc is always careful. He always gives good advice and never makes a mistake.

Is he really and truly the cleverest dwarf?

No, he is not really the *cleverest*; the other dwarfs are quite smart, too, but he is the one who has studied the most. Doc is a great reader and he loves books. We should all love books because all the knowledge that is in the world is in books. *Anything* we want to know we can find out from books.

We should listen carefully to the good advice which Doc gives us. This is what he says:

If you ask your father or your mother or your teacher, they will tell you what books you should read. Then you shouldn't let a single day pass without reading for a little while.

If you do as Doc says perhaps you'll grow up to be as wise as him. That would be nice, wouldn't it?

Peg-Leg-Pete

PEG LEG PETE was sure that he was the strongest person in the whole district. He could bend a bar of iron using only his hands, and he could break huge stones as if they were nuts.

Unfortunately his amazing strength had made him a great bully. He spent all day threatening and frightening everyone.

He used to do exercises to make himself even stronger. One day, he said to himself, "Today I shall amaze everyone with an exhibition of my strength. I am the strongest in the world."

Now Mickey heard this. And he accepted the challenge. "I'll take you on,"

he said. "Let's see what you can do."

Peg Leg Pete seemed like a giant beside Mickey!

But Mickey stood in front of him. The next second Peg Leg Pete was lying stretched out on the ground, groaning!

"How on earth were you able to knock me over without hitting me?" asked Peg Leg Pete in a dazed voice.

"Elementary, my dear Peg Leg!" said Mickey. "Strength alone is not worth anything. *I* am a master of Judo."

Moral: Skill is more valuable than strength.

Mickey's Exciting Sea Voyage

GOOFY HAD MADE A BOAT. "It's not exactly a marvel," he said to himself, "but at least it floats!"

Goofy invited his friend Mickey to come and take a trip with him. Mickey looked very doubtful. The boat didn't look at all safe, but he agreed.

Mickey and Goofy went on board and Goofy weighed anchor. When they were out on the open sea, the boat suddenly began to break up! First one plank came off then another and soon Mickey and Goofy were left clinging to a tiny raft.

Mickey fastened his shirt to a stick to make a sail. There was only a slight breeze and they hardly moved. "We'll never get back to harbour at this rate," said Mickey sadly.

Then, to his great horror, he saw that they were surrounded by sharks!

"Oh dear! What *shall* we do?" cried Goofy.

Just then Mickey spotted a ship on the horizon. "A sail! A sail!" he cried excitedly. Goofy and Mickey waved madly.

Slowly the ship steamed towards them and our friends were hauled aboard.

"I think I'll stick to dry land," said Goofy. "A sailor's life is too hard for me."

The School Concert

IT WAS NEARLY THE END of term at school and it was decided to give a concert for parents and for friends, so that the children could show everyone some of the things that they had learned.

Some recited beautiful poetry. Others performed a very funny play. There was a choir, too, which sang lots of gay little songs. There was a display of country dancing, too. But the highlight of the afternoon was a spectacular Gymnastic Display.

And do you know who were the stars of the show?

Why . . . Donald Duck's three little nephews, Huey, Dewey and Louie.

They performed a daring balancing act, just as if they had been born and bred in a circus.

How the audience clapped and cheered!

Uncle Donald was delighted. He smiled proudly at Mickey Mouse, Minnie and Goofy, who were cheering madly. Donald's little nephews were very clever, weren't they?

Moby Duck

NEARLY EVERYONE loves the sea. Many children dream of becoming sailors and sailing to far-off distant places, defying great storms and tempests.

Moby Duck had always loved the sea. As soon as he could, he got his own boat and he was very proud of it. It wasn't exactly a dashing transatlantic steamer. In fact, it had a very tumbledown appearance. But in spite of this, Moby Duck had sailed in her over all the seas of the world. He had even crossed the lonely Arctic seas to the icy regions of the Pole, through icebergs as tall as mountains. He had sailed through the warm seas of the tropics, too, calling at many lovely islands with golden beaches and tall palm-trees waving gently under the sun.

In fact, there wasn't a place in the world that he *hadn't* been to.

You might even see him when you're playing on the beach in the summertime. If you see a boat on the horizon, with a blue smoke stack and a gaily striped shade to keep off the sun, and a sailor at the wheel wearing a striped shirt and smoking a pipe, then you'll know it is Moby Duck.

Don't forget to wave to him. You'll make him very happy if you do because Moby Duck loves children. He'll probably give a great big blow on his hooter and wave back.

Wouldn't that be exciting?

Bambi and Falina

IT WAS SPRINGTIME at last! The cruel winter was over and all the animals of the wood felt gay and happy.

The carpet of snow had melted and the delicate little stems of the flowers were shooting up everywhere. The meadow was a splash of bright-coloured flowers which perfumed the breeze with a thousand sweet scents. The butterflies flittered gaily from flower to flower, the grasshoppers chirped merrily and the birds sang a sweet little song.

All the sufferings and hardships of winter were over. The warm sun shone gently, and all the animals felt so full of life that they wanted to dance and sing for joy.

Bambi especially felt very lively. He and Felina ran happily beside each other, through the wood and over the meadow. What a lovely time they had racing each other through the tall fresh grass.

Bambi just had to show off the strength of his lovely long legs. He bounded forward and jumped gracefully, high in the air, over a thicket. But he didn't realise that on the other side there was a pool of water . . .

Splash! Poor Bambi landed right among the bulrushes. How surprised he was!

And how Falina laughed! Then gently she licked the face of a very wet and a very cross Bambi.

But he was soon up and bounding away again.

Trip to Paris

ONE DAY THE GOOSE SISTERS, whose name was Gossip, decided to leave their quiet house in the country and pay a visit to their Uncle Drake who lived in Paris.

Now, this uncle often sent them letters telling all about the marvellous city and the wonderful things that happened there. So they were very curious to see for themselves.

After a long, tiring journey through France, they finally arrived at Paris where Uncle Drake was waiting to meet them.

"Oh, I'm starving," quacked one of the sisters. "Can we go and eat something?"

"I know just the place," quacked Uncle Drake. "The most famous restaurant in Paris. We'll have a wonderful meal."

So off they went to the restaurant. The manager was delighted to see them. He opened the door politely and with a big smile invited them in. They were just entering the door when suddenly Uncle Drake gave a frightened squawk and beat his wings frantically.

"Quick! get out!" he cried. And he rushed out through the door. The two frightened Gossip sisters followed him.

"What's the matter?" they cried, as soon as they were safely outside.

"I've just remembered that the speciality of the restaurant is Roast Goose," said Uncle Drake. "No wonder the manager welcomed us." The Gossip sisters understood at once that the big city was no place for them and they returned at once to their peaceful village.

They had a lucky escape, didn't they?

The Blue Balloon

ONE DAY, while he was walking through the wood, Winnie-the-Pooh spied a bees' nest high up in a tree.

"Where there are bees, there is honey," he said to himself, for he was a very clever little bear. "But the problem is, how do I reach it?"

He thought carefully for a long time. At last he went to his friend, Christopher, and asked if he could borrow his blue balloon. His plan was to float holding on to the balloon up into the tree, and so have a lovely feast of honey.

Christopher was quite happy to lend Pooh his balloon and, holding on to it, the bear rushed back to the tree.

Up, up, and up he floated. Right up to the very topmost branches of the tree.

He could *smell* the honey. He could even *see* it. But he couldn't *reach* it.

The bees were getting very angry. Buzz! Buzz! Buzz! Suddenly they left their nest and flew in a great cloud around Winnie-the-Pooh. And then they all flew at the balloon and stung it.

BANG! The balloon burst, and Winnie-the-Pooh fell down, down, down to the ground.

The little bear rubbed his sore head. "It's no good trying to get the better of those bees," he said to himself. "They're much cleverer than me!"

And they were, weren't they?

They'd just proved it.

Cats Don't Wear Diamonds

THIS IS A STORY about Thomas O'Malley, the alley cat, in the days before he came to live with the aristocats in their big old mansion.

Life was very hard in the back streets where Thomas O'Malley lived. But he was a tough cat and had learned to look after himself.

It was often very difficult to find food, but Thomas O'Malley never gave up. He used to go down the dark alleys at the back of the smart restaurants and sit by the gratings over the kitchens. At least he could enjoy the heavenly smells!

One of his favourite tricks was to jump on the huge dustbins and scrummage about inside. He found many tasty titbits that way. Pieces of juicy fish, a few yards of spaghetti. An odd meatball or two. And many beautiful bones.

Late one night he went down to his favourite, Le Petit Montmartre restaurant. It was one of the smartest and most expensive in Paris. He was sure to find something delicious there.

The restaurant had been long shut and was in darkness. The moonlight glimmered on the row of dustbins. As usual, Pierre the Cook had been too lazy to put the lids back on.

Thomas O'Malley jumped on the first one and had a quick look round. "Miaow!" he cried. "Not much here."

He jumped on the second. This was better. "Miaow! My favourite dish! Oysters!" he cried, licking his lips. "Now for a little of the main course," he cried, his whiskers twitching eagerly. He was lucky. The third dustbin held some delicious bits of steak.

"Ah! Steak Bonaparte!" he cried. "My favourite," and he tucked in heartily.

"Now, just a little pudding," said O'Malley. "And I've had a feast fit for a King of Cats."

So speaking, he jumped on the fourth dustbin. He scrummaged but there didn't seem to be anything. Not a single sausage!

He put down his paw deep into the dustbin and brought up a paper napkin. He gave it a shake and something gleaming tinkled to the ground. "If that ain't the cat's whiskers!" cried O'Malley in astonishment. "If I'm not mistaken, them's *diamonds*."

And indeed they were. A long glittering bracelet of diamonds, sparkling as if they were on fire.

O'Malley jumped to the ground and picked up the bracelet in his mouth.

Diamonds in a dustbin—whoever heard of such a thing?

"They're mighty pretty," he murmured to himself. "But not much use to a cat. You can't *eat* a diamond, for instance."

Still holding the bracelet in his mouth, O'Malley made his way to his modest little room. He hid the bracelet under the floorboard. It was much too pretty to leave in a dustbin.

The weeks passed by and O'Malley quite forgot about the bracelet. Until July, when his friend Scat Cat decided to throw a party.

"You must come and bring a girl-friend, O'Malley," said Scat Cat with a grin.

Scat Cat's parties were famous, for his jazz band was the best in all Paris. Cool cats came from miles around.

O'Malley decided to take Chantal, the pretty little half-Siamese. "Here's a little trinket for you to wear," said O'Malley, throwing to her the diamond bracelet he had found.

"Miaow! Miaow!" cried Chantal in delight, as she fastened it round her throat.

They were just passing the front of Le Petit Montmartre. A lady and a gentleman had just got out of a taxi and were going up the steps of the restaurant. The two cats stopped to let them pass.

"Why, Henri!" cried the lady in astonishment. "There's my bracelet!"

"Take it off, quick," whispered O'Malley to Chantal.

Chantal unfastened the bracelet and it fell to the floor at the gentleman's feet.

He stooped and picked up the bracelet. "Why, so it is!" he cried. "Where on earth did it come from?"

"It seemed to me that the cat was wearing it," said the lady.

"Nonsense," said the gentleman, "cats don't wear diamonds."

"I was *sure* I lost it in the restaurant," said the lady. "Perhaps the clever cat found it." And she bent down and patted O'Malley's head.

"Wait," said the gentleman. "They deserve a reward."

He darted into the restaurant and soon returned with a plate of Pierre's most delicious fish. "There, tuck in, cats."

And they did. It was delicious.

"Never mind, Chantal," said Thomas O'Malley when the meal was over. "The gentleman's quite right. Cats don't wear diamonds."

But Chantal wasn't so sure. "Miaow!" she said, rather sadly.

Jelly

PLUTO WAS ON HOLIDAY at the seaside with Mickey Mouse. Every morning, before Mickey was awake, he used to go down to the beach. He liked it there because there were so many exciting smells. He had a lovely time, sniffing the seaweed, paddling in the little pools and playing with the little waves.

One sunny morning he was running over the golden sand when he suddenly stopped. "Whoof! Whoof!" he cried excitedly. There, before him, was a big, wobbly JELLY.

Pluto stopped in surprise. Now there was one thing he really loved, and that was jelly. But he had never seen jelly on a beach before. Usually they had it for tea with fruit and cream.

Pluto stopped and eyed the jelly suspiciously. "It's funny-looking jelly," he thought to himself.

Now, Pluto was a very careful dog. He wasn't going to take any chances. Slowly he backed away. Then, crouching to the ground he growled as fiercely as he could, showing all his teeth, "GRRRR!"

The jelly didn't move. "Well, it's not alive, that's for sure," said Pluto. In fact,

the jelly didn't move. It just stood there, swaying gently in the breeze.

Pluto sat down near the jelly and watched it. Slowly his little black nose began to twitch. "Really, it is disgraceful," said Pluto. "Fancy leaving jelly on the beach."

Pluto closed his eyes but his nose went on twitching. "Oh, I do feel hungry!" he said to himself. "It must be time for breakfast."

"He opened one eye. The jelly was still there. "Well, it doesn't *belong* to anyone," said Pluto. "Nobody leaves jelly on a beach if they want it."

He opened the other eye. "I wonder what *sort* of jelly it is," he said. "Lemon is my favourite. It looks sort of lemony."

Slowly he put out his tongue. "Just one little lick," he said to himself. The tip of his tongue touched the jelly. "Hmm! not much of a taste."

He looked around him. The beach was

empty. He opened his mouth wide and bit at the jelly. . . .

Pluto gave a great squeal of fright and fell back on to the sand. PLOP! His poor little nose was on fire! Quickly he ran to the sea and ducked his head into the cool water. Ah! That was better!

His little nose felt HUGE. He looked at his reflection. It *was* huge! And bright red!

"WHOOF! WHOOF!" he barked angrily. Who had ever heard of a jelly that could *sting*! He'd never eat another jelly as long as he lived.

Shaking with shock, Pluto crawled out of the sea. This beach was much too dangerous. He'd go back to the hotel where it was safer. He bounded across the beach as fast as his trembling legs could carry him.

The little jellyfish smiled happily. Fancy a great big brute of a dog trying to eat *her*. That would teach him a lesson!

Bambi Finds Something Odd

ONE DAY when he was playing in the forest, Bambi, the little deer, noticed something odd lying among the leaves. He poked at it with his nose and sniffed at it. He had no idea what it was.

Then the bear came along. He looked at the strange thing, too. He rolled it over and over with his big paws. But he couldn't think what it was. He called the other animals to come and look at it. Not one of them had ever seen anything like it before. No one knew where it had come from or how it had got there.

The ferret said, "It's plain that it's the bark of a tree."

"Oh, no," said a rabbit, "It must be the skin of some fruit."

Then a little mouse said, "I think it is the shell of a nut."

But a little bird twittered, "It's not that at all. It's some kind of a bird's nest. Look, here's the hole for the bird to go in. Here is the deep part for the eggs. It *must* be a bird's nest."

Then a tiny little beetle said, "You're all wrong." He pointed to the long, thin thing that came out of the strange object, "Look at this long root. It is some kind of plant, of course."

And so the animals went on arguing angrily, each thinking that he was right.

"I know," said Bambi, twitching his little velvety nose. "Let's ask the owl. *He* will know."

The old owl was sitting in a tree nearby, watching the animals quarrelling. "If you will all keep quiet, I will tell you what it is. I have seen more of these things than you can count."

The animals stopped arguing and waited quietly for the owl to go on.

"It's a man's shoe," said the owl in a very proud voice.

"A *what*?" cried all the animals in surprise.

"What is a man, and what is a shoe?" asked Bambi curiously.

"A man," said the owl, ruffling his feathers importantly, "is a thing with two legs. He is like a bird, but he has no feathers. He can walk like us. He can eat like us. He can talk like us. But he can do much more than we can."

How can a thing with only two legs do more than we can with four legs?" growled the bear. "It's not true, of course."

"Of course it's not true!" screeched the birds. "How can there be a thing with two legs without feathers?"

"Well," cried the owl, "it *is* true. A man makes things like this. He calls them shoes and he puts them on his feet."

"Not true! Not true!" shouted all the animals. "We know that such things are not worn on the feet. You are not fit to live with us. You must leave the forest."

So they chased the poor owl out of the forest. "It *is* true, whatever you say," screeched the owl angrily, as he flew away.

Bambi stood still, staring down at the strange object. "Perhaps it *is* true," he whispered. Then he looked down at his four little brown hooves, "My hooves are like little shoes. Why shouldn't a man have shoes, too?"

The Singing Whale

ONE DAY a sensational piece of news appeared in all the newspapers of the world. A fisherman had seen a whale who could sing opera!

At once many whaling men sailed off to try to capture this whale. For he would be worth a lot of money.

At last they heard the sound of singing! There was the singing whale! They stopped their boats to listen. The whale sang many songs in a loud, beautiful voice, and the listening sailors were lost in wonder and admiration.

Just then the captain of the nearest boat raised his harpoon.

"No! No!" cried the sailors. "You mustn't kill him! We'd rather hear him singing as we sail over these seas."

The captain lowered his harpoon. The whale was so delighted that it sang many lovely arias from famous operas.

When it had finished, all the sailors clapped heartily.

Now, whenever a ship or a fishing-boat sails there, they all stop a while to listen to the beautiful songs of the singing whale.

Perhaps *you* will hear him one day when you make a voyage across the sea.

The Holidays

SCHOOL WOULD SOON be breaking up for the holidays and all the children were talking about where they were going to go.

Mickey Mouse's two little nephews spent hours and hours talking about the places they liked best.

One day they almost had a fight about it, because they both wanted to go to different places.

"I like the sea best," said Ferdie. "It's lovely to play on the beach. We can build some huge sandcastles and we can swim in the lovely cool water. And we can go out in a boat, and perhaps do some fishing. We're sure to catch lots of crabs. Yes! We'll go to the sea!"

"Oh no!" said Morty, "we'll go to the mountains! We can climb the rocks and pick lovely wild flowers, and see the flocks of sheep in the fields high above the valleys."

"No!" said Ferdie angrily. "To the sea!"

"No!" said Morty in a terrible voice. "To the mountains!"

Ferdie put down his toy aeroplane and Morty left his scooter. They were just about to have a fight when Mickey appeared.

"Stop this nonsense!" he said crossly. "It's no good you two arguing. My mind is made up. I haven't got much money to spare this year, so we're going to spend the summer with Goofy on his farm."

Ferdie and Morty looked at each other and smiled. They didn't really mind. In fact, they *loved* Goofy's farm.

The Prince of the Forest

LOOK AT THIS LOVELY PICTURE of Bambi. Isn't he a wonderful sight?

Many years have passed since Bambi was born. Then he was only a little weak creature, but now he is a beautiful stag. Look at his strong body and powerful horns.

It is Bambi's job to look after all the other animals in the wood. All day long he passes through the wood, helping anyone who is in trouble, especially the small, weak animals. They are all in his care and he looks after them well, for he remembers the time when *he* was little and frightened by all kinds of things. But now he is the Prince of the Forest.

But it wasn't easy to become the Prince of the Forest. Bambi had to learn many things. He listened carefully to his mother and to the wiser animals and he had to spend much time at his lessons. Often he wanted to run away and play, but he knew that he would only be safe in the wood if he knew how to look after himself. Now Bambi is glad that he knows many things, for he has a very important job. He must be a good, brave leader for that is his duty.

Bambi can teach us all a lesson. We must all work hard like him if we want to get on in the world and have an important job one day.

Thumper's Girl-Friend

THUMPER RABBIT was sure that he would never get married. Whenever he heard that a friend of his was going to be married, he burst into laughter. *He* would never do such a silly thing.

But one day, as he was hopping merrily through the forest, he suddenly stopped still. There before him on the path stood the most beautiful rabbit that he had ever seen.

This lovely creature stood blinking her eyes in the sunshine. She had big soft eyes and long sweeping eyelashes. Her long pointed ears twitched gracefully.

At once Thumper Rabbit fell in love with her. "I must marry her," he whispered to himself. And off he scampered to tell Bambi about it.

Bambi was very amused. "Why have you changed your mind so suddenly?" he asked.

Thumper Rabbit sighed deeply and replied, "It's a wise person who changes his opinion."

"Well," said Bambi, with a twinkle in his eye, "You'd better ask her, then."

So Thumper Rabbit bounded away happily through the wood. He met the lovely rabbit again and they had a very happy time playing together.

The weeks passed by. At last Thumper Rabbit plucked up his courage and asked her to marry him.

The little rabbit blushed sweetly and whispered, "Yes."

Thumper Rabbit's little tail twitched happily. How glad he was that *he* was wise enough to change his mind.

Hobbies

DONALD DUCK'S THREE little nephews are often in trouble because they are so mischievous. But sometimes they are very good and quiet.

Donald has found a good way of keeping them busy and happy. He has encouraged each of them to have a hobby. Often, in the evenings, the little ducks spend many pleasant hours with their different hobbies.

Huey collects stamps. This is a very interesting hobby and it is also useful because it teaches you a lot about geography. Huey has lots of stamps. He has some from every country in the world and he sticks them into a special book.

Some are very beautiful with lovely pictures of birds and flowers and people.

Dewey collects all kinds of stones and mineral ores. He spends hours and hours looking for new ones to add to his collection. This is a very interesting hobby, too, for you can learn all about geology. You can find interesting stones everywhere—by rivers, in the fields, or near the sea.

Louie has a wonderful collection of postcards. He has postcards of places all over the world. Whenever someone sends him a card, he adds it to his collection which he keeps in a big cardboard box. He has postcards of big cities with famous buildings and statues, and of little villages —all from far-off countries. One day he hopes to visit many of these places.

Have *you* got an interesting hobby?

Jaq and Gus

JAQ, GUS and the other little mice who live in Cinderella's house have a terrible problem. His name is Lucifer.

Lucifer is a big fat evil cat. He spends all his time chasing the unhappy mice and making their lives a perfect misery.

Fortunately, Jaq and Gus and their mouse friends have two very important allies without whom life in that house would be impossible.

These are Cinderella and Bruno.

Cinderella is very fond of the mice and helps them as much as she can. She always keeps tasty little bits of cheese in the kitchen for them. Bruno is a big hunt-ing dog, the only one Lucifer is afraid of. Whenever Lucifer sees him, he runs away as quickly as he can and he only comes back when Bruno has gone.

When the mice want to go out to find something to eat, they first have to make sure that Cinderella or Bruno is there. Then they feel safe. That Lucifer is very sly. He is always hanging about, looking for the mice and waiting to pounce on them.

But he hasn't ever caught a single mouse. Not *one*!

And he won't, either. Cinderella and Bruno will see to that!

Figaro
Disappears

ONE DAY, AS PINOCCHIO was coming home from school, he saw two men coming out of his house. They looked very angry. Mr. Gepetto stood in his doorway with a very worried look on his face.

"What's the matter, daddy?" asked Pinocchio.

"Those men are my best customers," replied the old man. "I mended some clocks for them, but they have just brought one back because it doesn't work at all. And it's a very expensive one. And, as if that wasn't enough, Figaro has disappeared. I can't find him anywhere. I'm just going out into the street to look for him."

Pinocchio spent all the afternoon looking for the kitten, but there was no sign of him.

Later on, when Gepetto went out to look for the kitten again, Pinocchio decided to look at the big clock. Perhaps he could find out what was wrong with it. Perhaps he could even mend it.

He opened the case, and what do you think he saw?

Figaro the cat!

"Miaow! Miaow!" cried Figaro, as he jumped on to Pinocchio's lap.

And at once the clock began to work.

Tick! Tock! Tick! Tock! Tick! Tock!

How pleased Gepetto was when he returned!

"Silly pussy!" he said, "but clever, clever Pinocchio!"

Brer Fox Cleans The Chimney

BRER RABBIT was very angry. He just couldn't get his fire to light. He prodded the coals with his poker, and a thick cloud of yellow smoke blew into his face. "Oh dear! Oh dear!" he coughed and spluttered. "What is the matter with this old fire?"

Brer Rabbit decided to go and ask Brer Bear about it. "He'll know what to do," he said to himself.

Brer Bear was sitting in front of a beautiful fire. The coals were glowing red and pretty little yellow flames danced all over them.

"Oh, it's a great pleasure to sit by a fire like this," said Brer Rabbit, holding out his hands to get them warm. "My house is so cold."

"I expect your chimney needs sweeping," said Brer Bear calmly. He knew all about things like that.

"Sweeping?" cried Brer Rabbit in surprise. "But I haven't got a long brush. Where can I possibly get one from?"

All the way home Brer Rabbit pulled at his whiskers, thinking and thinking. But he was a mighty smart Rabbit, and at last he had an idea.

The next day he went to call on Brer Fox. "Excuse me," he said politely when Brer Fox answered the door, "But I do believe there's a great big chicken stuck in my chimney."

"A chicken, did you say?" murmured Brer Fox, stroking his chin thoughtfully.

"Indeed," said Brer Rabbit. "I can hear him squawking. I thought you might like to catch him."

Now, if there was one thing Brer Fox loved it was a tasty chicken dinner. "Well, that's mighty kind of you, Brer Rabbit," he said. "I'll come and take a look."

So off they went to Brer Rabbit's house. "Excuse the dust covers," said Brer Rabbit. "I'm just doing some spring-cleaning." Then he peered up the chimney, "I can just see his tail feathers," he cried. "If you were to go up, Brer Fox, I'm sure you could catch him."

So, huffing and puffing and grunting and groaning, Brer Fox climbed the chimney. Great clouds of black soot came floating down. Brer Fox's bushy tail was just like a thick brush and as it moved from side to side it swept the chimney beautifully.

"I can't see any chicken," yelled Brer Fox, nearly choking.

"Just a bit farther," cried Brer Rabbit. "I expect he's flown up higher."

By this time Brer Fox had reached the top of the chimney. How surprised he was when his head popped out of the chimney pot. There was only one thing to do—and that was to slither down again.

How angry Brer Fox was! "You wait till I get hold of you, you miserable Rabbit," he yelled.

But of course Brer Rabbit wasn't in sight. He hid behind a bush until Brer Fox, covered in soot from head to foot, and grumbling furiously, had passed.

"Now I'll have such a cosy fire," he cried happily. "Thank you, Brer Fox, for cleaning my chimney!"

The Spell that Wouldn't Stop

ONE FINE MORNING Miss Eglantine Price looked around the sitting-room of her pretty little cottage and sighed, "Oh dear! This spring sunshine shows up all the dust. Look at the dirty windows! And I do believe that's a cobweb on the beams. I shall have to do some spring-cleaning."

"It's a pity you don't know a spell to help you," said Paul. "There's no point in being a witch if you don't get any *advantage* out of it."

"That's quite true," said Miss Price. "But I don't know any spells for spring-cleaning. After all, I'm only *learning* to be a witch and I don't know *everything* yet."

"Why don't you look in your note-book?" said Carrie. "There might be something useful there."

Miss Price took out her little notebook and turned the pages. "I don't think so," she said. "Now, let me see . . . Spells for making things small . . . spells for making things big . . ." She turned a few more pages. "Spells to make things move all by themselves . . . ah! . . . what about this? A spell to clean things quickly. Now *that* might do." Eagerly, Miss Price read the spell.

"Can you do it?" asked Paul excitedly.

"Well, we'll try," said Miss Price. "I'll need three cloths, a duster for the furniture, a floor-cloth for the floor, and a rag for the windows."

Carrie hurried to the kitchen, found

the cloths and laid them on the floor in front of Miss Price.

Miss Price picked up each of the cloths in turn, waved it in the air and whispered the magic words. "Now clean as quick as you can, and don't stop!" she cried.

For a moment nothing happened.

"Look!" Carrie murmured, "The duster is moving!"

"And the floor-cloth!" said Charlie.

"And the rag!" said Paul, in a hushed whisper.

Slowly the three cloths rose from the floor. They moved faster and faster now. The duster flew to the furniture. It polished the oak table until you could see your face in it. Then it flew to the chair and polished it in seconds. Then off it went to the bookcase dusting all the way.

The floor-cloth spun round the floor until it shone. Then it darted into the kitchen. A few minutes later it flew back and up the stairs.

The rag flew out of the door and almost at once they saw it flying over the outside of the windows. Round and round, until the glass sparkled.

"Oh, how wonderful!" said Miss Price, clapping her hands. "They're saving us hours and hours of hard work."

Now the floor-cloth had followed the duster up the stairs, and the rag had disappeared to do the upstairs windows.

Soon the duster and floor-cloth came flying down the stairs. They had cleaned everything.

"Finished so soon!" said Miss Price in amazement, looking at her watch. The furniture gleamed. The mirrors shone. All the ornaments and knick-knacks were clean and shiny.

"Come and see the kitchen," said Carrie. "It's marvellous!" And indeed it was! The cooker was cleaner than Miss Price had ever seen it! The refrigerator

sparkled. The shelves were all tidy. Even the dish-rack and the sink had been washed.

"Oh, it's lovely," said Miss Price, going back to the sitting-room. "The cottage is spotless. You can stop now."

But the cloths went on flying about. The rag had come in again and was just finishing the inside of the windows.

The duster was busy polishing the apples on the sideboard.

The floor-cloth was wiping the coal in the scuttle.

Suddenly the rag flew straight at Paul and started polishing his face!

"Stop it! Stop it!" cried Miss Price, but then the duster flew over her face so that she couldn't speak.

"That's enough! Please stop!" she cried frantically as the duster started dusting her hair.

But it was no use. The three cloths went whirling about, until the children were dusted from top-to-toe. Then they started cleaning everything again.

"Oh dear! What shall we do?" said Miss Price, almost in tears.

"Don't you know a spell for making things stop?" asked Paul who, because he was the smallest, had been dusted three times by now.

"No, I'm afraid I don't," said Miss Price, looking frantically through her notebook. "But wait . . . here's a spell for making things follow. I'll have to use that. Where's my broom?"

Paul rushed to the little cupboard where Miss Price kept her broom and brought it out. "Here it is," he cried.

Quickly Miss Price climbed on. Looking at her notebook she chanted the magic words. Then off she flew through the open door. SWOOOSH!!

The children watched in amazement. The three cloths flew in a straight line after Miss Price! Up, up they climbed, high into the sky.

"Thank goodness!" said Paul, whose face was shining from being dusted so much.

Hours later Miss Price returned, shivering a little with the cold. "The last I saw of them," she said, "they were polishing the moon and the stars. There's going to be a beautiful bright moon to-night!"

King Louie

KING LOUIE is a simply enormous orang-utan who is the King of the Monkeys. He is very, very strong, the strongest of all, although he is not very bright.

Now, Mowgli, the little Man Cub, was very curious. He wanted to find out if King Louie really was as strong as everyone said he was. So one day he marched off into the jungle, to the Ruined City where King Louie lived.

Mowgli found King Louie sitting on his throne, a crowd of chattering monkeys around him.

"What do you want, boy?" asked King Louie as he lazily peeled a banana.

"I've come to find out if you are really strong," said Mowgli. "How would you like to have a fight with me?"

The only answer King Louie made was to pick up Mowgli with one little finger!

Mowgli screamed and kicked his legs and shook his arms angrily, but King Louie only laughed and said, "It's stupid to challenge the strongest, my boy, especially if they haven't picked a quarrel with you."

King Louie was right, of course.

"Do you agree?" the Monkey King asked Mowgli, who was still struggling.

"Yes! Yes! Put me down!" yelled Mowgli.

King Louie dropped Mowgli to the ground. "Let that be a lesson to you, my boy," said King Louie.

It was. Mowgli never picked a quarrel with King Louie again.

91

Naughty Lampwick

LAMPWICK IS NOT a nice boy at all. In fact, he is very, very naughty. He is always getting into trouble, he never studies his lessons and sometimes he is even a little cruel. Because of this he hasn't any friends. Nobody wants to play with such a stupid boy.

But Pinocchio was sure that *he* could make Lampwick a good boy and he decided to try to be friends with him. So one day he invited Lampwick to tea.

Lampwick was quite good while they were having tea, but afterwards he found some ice skates in Pinocchio's toy cupboard and put them on.

"But you can't skate!" said Pinocchio.

"There isn't any ice inside a house!"

"But I want to skate," said Lampwick. "And I'll show you how to do it."

He climbed on to the table and began to skate on the shiny, polished surface.

"Don't do that!" cried Pinocchio. "You'll ruin it! Stop! Stop!"

But wicked Lampwick would not stop. Round and round he skated, leaving terrible deep scratches on the table.

When Gepetto came home and saw what had happened, he was very cross.

"Don't you ever play with that boy again!" he scolded.

So Pinocchio never did. And now Lampwick feels very, very lonely.

Kanga and Roo

DO YOU REMEMBER Kanga and Roo, who are great friends of Winnie-the-Pooh and Christopher Robin?

Well, Mummy Kanga, like all mothers, always takes great care of her little son, Roo, and tries to make him happy.

Can you see them in the picture? To-day they have come out for a walk in the wood. When they had been walking for a time Little Roo felt tired and he asked his mother to make a swing for him.

"But we haven't any ropes," she said.

Little Roo looked so disappointed that Kanga said, "We'll try to make some."

She found some strong ivy creepers and a nice piece of wood. First she tied the creepers to the wood and then she tied the creepers to a branch of a tree. What a lovely swing it made! And it was quite safe because Little Roo is really very small and not very heavy. Can you see the swing in the picture?

Roo is really enjoying himself, isn't he? He loves it when Kanga pushes him high and he flies through the air.

"Oh, this is lovely!" cries the little kangaroo. "Can we come here again?"

"Why, yes!" said Kanga, pleased that her little son was so happy. "We'll come as often as you like."

93

Summer Games

FERDIE AND MORTY, Mickey Mouse's little nephews, are spending their holidays on Goofy's farm in the country.

They are having a wonderful time. There are so many interesting things to see and they think of lots of exciting things to do.

One day they decided to play a game of "Cowboys". They put on the cowboy clothes which they had had for Christmas, found a strong rope and went off to the meadow.

"Let's play lassooing!" cried Ferdie.

"Yes!" said Morty. "Just like real cowboys."

But, of course, they had to try to lassoo something.

"Let's see if we can catch that little lamb," cried Ferdie.

They both ran after the lamb and Ferdie threw the lassoo around its neck. How the poor little thing struggled!

Morty pulled the rope tight and the frightened little lamb stood still, bleating pitifully.

Just then Mickey came into the meadow and heard the sad cries of the lamb. At once he saw what had happened.

"You naughty boys!" he cried, rushing to the rescue. Quickly he undid the rope. The little lamb bleated his thanks and then ran away.

"What a naughty thing to do!" said Mickey crossly. "You must always be careful when you play and never hurt anyone."

Ferdie and Morty were very sorry, and they never did it again.

A Day at the Beach

ONE SUNNY DAY Donald decided to take his three little nephews to the beach.

How excited they were! They all helped Donald to pack the car. They put in their fishing-rods, their buckets and spades, their rubber beds for floating on the water and, of course, their bathing-suits. Then Donald fixed their little boat to the back of the car.

Soon they were off! Laughing and singing merrily because they *loved* the seaside.

As soon as they reached the seaside, Donald unfastened the boat. The three little ducks helped him to push it over the beach into the sea. Then they all clambered aboard. Donald started the engine and up and down the beach they chugged, waving to the bathers in the water.

"Oh, that water looks so inviting!" cried Donald. "Who's coming for a swim?"

"We are!" cried the little ducks, for they *loved* swimming.

Soon they all had their bathing-suits on and were splashing happily in the cool water.

Then they had a race to see who would be first to reach a rock which was sticking up out of the water.

Of course they can all swim very well. In fact, they have been swimming for a long time for they first learned when they were very small.

But all the same, they are always very careful and never go far from the beach.

You must always be careful in the sea, mustn't you? For danger can occur when you least expect it.

Winnie-The-Pooh Comes to Tea

WINNIE-THE-POOH is a very greedy little bear. In fact, he is the greediest little bear in all the world. He's got such a sweet tooth that he just cannot stop eating honey. All day long he goes around looking for honey and hoping to be invited to share some with someone.

One day he went to call on his friend Rabbit in his burrow. Rabbit was just going to have tea and so he invited the little bear to have some, too.

When Winnie-the-Pooh saw the lovely honey that Rabbit had, he sat down at the table at once.

Rabbit put some honey on the little bear's plate. In a second it was gone! Rabbit put some more . . . and some more . . . *and* some more.

Winnie-the-Pooh ate . . . and ate . . . ate and . . . until he could hardly move.

"Oh, thank you, friend Rabbit," said Winnie-the-Pooh when all the honey-jars were empty. "That was a lovely little snack."

"*Snack*?" cried Rabbit crossly. "You've eaten my whole store of honey."

"Well, it was very nice," said Pooh Bear, rubbing his tummy. "I really enjoyed it. Now I'd better get off home."

But do you know what had happened?

Winnie-the-Pooh had got so fat he couldn't get through Rabbit's door!

"Serve you right," said Rabbit. "You'll have to starve for a while."

So poor Pooh had to wait for a whole week without touching a mouthful of food until he was slim enough to go through the door again!

Ferdinand The Bull

FERDINAND WAS A MOST unusual bull. In fact, he wasn't like other bulls at all.

Although he was very strong with powerful horns, he wasn't at all fierce. He hated rough games and fighting as the other bulls did. The thing he loved best was to smell the pretty flowers in the meadow. He was very, very gentle and liked a peaceful life.

One day some rough men came to the meadow where Ferdinand lived. They caught him and tied him up with thick ropes and took him away and sold him to a man who put him in a big cage. A few days later the man took him to the bull-ring.

"He's a fine bull," said his new owner. "He will fight well."

But do you know what Ferdinand did?

Nothing! Yes, nothing! Absolutely nothing!

He just sat down in the middle of the arena and smiled at all the people.

The matador took out his big sword and tried to make Ferdinand charge, but Ferdinand didn't want to fight. He didn't even want to walk about. He saw a lovely rose lying on the sand and began to sniff it happily.

How the crowd laughed!

"Take him away!" cried the owner angrily. And some men tied Ferdinand up again and pulled him out of the ring.

Ferdinand was very glad to be back in the meadow. Since then he has lived there happily and quietly sniffing the flowers. The most daring thing he does is to chase butterflies!

The Little Black Lamb

ONCE UPON A TIME, there was a little boy called Emilio who had a beautiful little lamb. Now, this lamb was very unusual because she was completely black, without a spot of white anywhere.

One day Emilio decided to take his lamb to the Fair which was held every year. Perhaps she would win a prize!

As soon as they arrived, Emilio shut up his lamb safely in the stable so that he could go off and look at the Fair.

The little lamb felt very sad, all by herself in the stable. She wanted to see all the pretty things in the Fair, too. She pushed hard at the door and to her surprise it opened. Quickly she trotted away.

What exciting things she saw all around her! The Fair was full of people who pushed and jostled each other. She had never seen such a hustle and bustle. And what a terrible noise there was! Sirens screamed, bells rang, and there was a great clash and clatter as the Big Wheel went round. Then suddenly a great rocket went off—WHOOSH! Then another . . . and another . . . It was all too much for the little lamb. She was absolutely terrified and hurried back to the stable.

How pleased she was when Emilio came back and how pleased Emilio was when his little lamb won first prize!

He bought her lots of nice things to eat and the little lamb was very happy.

"I'll never run away again," she bleated.

And she never did.

Toot the Little Tug

TOOT, THE LITTLE TUG, thought his father had a wonderful job. He looked on proudly when the big tug towed the huge transatlantic liners into port.

How he longed to do the same!

One day he decided to try. But a terrible thing happened. He made a silly mistake and the big boat he was pulling banged against the side of the harbour. The Authorities were very angry. They told him he could never sail in those waters again and they sent him away.

Poor Toot felt very sad.

One night there was a terrible storm. The waves were as high as mountains and the rain slashed down. Toot could see a ship in trouble. Quickly he chugged towards it. The captain threw him a line and Toot tugged the ship through the rough sea safely into the harbour.

How proud Toot's father was!

The Authorities were very pleased, too. They forgave Toot for his past mistake, and even gave him an award for his bravery.

Now Toot is very happy. And he always does what he is told. Sometimes he helps his father, but he never tows a ship by himself. There will be plenty of time to do that when he is bigger.

The Three Caballeros

DO YOU REMEMBER Panchito, the brave cockerel who lived in Mexico?

Well, this Panchito had a magic flying blanket. Panchito could travel on it to any place in the world which he wanted to see.

One day, Panchito invited his friends Donald Duck and Pedro, who lived in Brazil, to come and visit him. He hadn't seen them for a very long time.

When the two friends arrived they were very interested to see Panchito's magic blanket.

"Step on!" cried Panchito. "I'll give you a little demonstration!"

So the three friends stepped on to the blanket. SWOOSH! At once it flew up into the air.

"I'll show you my country," cried Panchito.

What a wonderful journey they had! Panchito pointed out to them all the beautiful things of Mexico—the high, snow-topped mountains, the wide rivers, the villages and the big cities.

"How marvellous it is to see the world from up high," quacked Donald.

Panchito fired his guns excitedly.

"It's fantastic," croaked Pedro, the parrot.

Over and over the country the blanket flew. How surprised the birds were when they saw them.

"How quickly the time has passed," squawked Pedro, for it was almost dark when at last they returned to Panchito's house.

"We'll visit some other countries one day," promised Panchito.

Chip 'n' Dale Fool Donald

CHIP 'N' DALE, the little chipmunks, were feeling very miserable. They were fed up with all the practical jokes that Donald played on them.

He never gave them a moment's peace. He was always thinking up new ways to tease and annoy them. Only yesterday they had been playing with their big brightly coloured football when Donald had come along and given it a huge kick. The ball had flown through the air a long, long way and Chip 'n' Dale had to run after it because they didn't want to lose it. The ball landed in the bushes and it was hours before they found it. And when they finally did, they were covered in scratches. Chip 'n' Dale thought and thought of a way to get their own back. At last they had an idea.

Chip painted a big round stone the same colours as the ball. Then they put the stone in the middle of the lawn so that Donald would see it.

Donald came along a little later. When he saw the ball he stopped. Then he took a little run and aimed a great kick at the ball.

"Awwwwww!" Donald cried. Clutching his poor foot, he hopped all around the garden.

How Chip 'n' Dale laughed! Donald's foot hurt so much that he couldn't walk for weeks. Chip 'n' Dale were able to play happily without being disturbed.

Even when his foot was better, Donald left the chipmunks alone. He had learned his lesson!

Mowgli and The Elephants

EVERY DAY, VERY EARLY in the morning, the herd of elephants marched through the jungle.

Their leader was a huge beast called Colonel Hathi. Years ago he had served in the Army, but he seemed to have forgotten that he was now retired for he still ordered the herd about as if they were soldiers.

On this particular morning, Mowgli and Bagheera the Panther were fast asleep on the bough of a tree. Suddenly there was a terrible noise. It was the dreadful trumpeting of the elephants. Mowgli and Bagheera awoke with a start.

"It's those boring old elephants again," growled Bagheera crossly. "This jungle is becoming impossible! One just cannot get a decent night's sleep here."

Mowgli sat up sleepily and rubbed his eyes. "You're right, Bagheera," he said. "We'll have to think of a way of punishing them."

Mowgli and Bagheera thought carefully. They could hear the elephants crashing through the jungle. The noise was as loud as thunder and it came closer and closer.

"I know just the thing!" cried Mowgli suddenly. He stood up and, imitating the voice of Colonel Hathi, cried:

"PLATOON! HALT!"

The elephants were not expecting this order. The one in front stopped suddenly in surprise and all the elephants behind bumped into each other . . . one after the other.

What a sight it was!

The elephants were in complete confusion.

The Colonel was purple in the face. "SQUAD! ATTENTION!" he cried.

But it was too late. The elephants were a squirming mass of legs and trunks. Finally they all collapsed in a heap, rubbing their sore trunks.

How Mowgli and Bagheera laughed!

They laughed so much that their sides ached.

"That'll teach you!" yelled Mowgli.

"Go and play at parading somewhere else," growled Bagheera.

Slowly the elephants got to their feet. Colonel Hathi tried to order them into a straight line but the elephants were too cross. One by one they straggled off through the jungle.

"SQUAD! ATTENTION!" cried Colonel Hathi.

But no one took the slightest notice.

From that moment on, the peacefulness of the jungle was not disturbed by the loud trumpetings and tramplings of the elephants. At least, not until the sun was high in the sky and all the animals were wide awake.

Donald and Daisy Meet a Ghost

DONALD DUCK AND DAISY were on holiday in Scotland. They were staying at an old gloomy castle beside a lake.

"Do you think there's a ghost?" asked Daisy nervously one evening, as they were having dinner.

"Quack! Quack!" cried Donald, who was eating his soup. "There should be. This hotel is very expensive and a ghost should be among the attractions."

"Oh, I hope not!" whispered Daisy, fearfully. "I'd be terrified!"

"Don't worry, Daisy," cried Donald. "Remember, I'm here to protect you." This was really very brave of Donald, because he had never seen a ghost either.

Later that night, Donald was getting ready for bed when his door burst open. It was Daisy, her face as white as a sheet and her teeth chattering with fright. "It's a G-G-G-GHOST!" she stammered.

"Where is it?" cried Donald, trying to be brave. "What's it doing?"

"It's sitting on my bed!" cried Daisy.

"I was just going to put out the light and get into bed when I saw it. What are we going to do?"

"Do?" cried Donald, scratching his head. "I don't rightly know. What *do* you *do* about ghosts?"

"Well, we can't leave it there," cried Daisy. "It's *my* room, and I'm sleepy and want to go to bed."

"I'd better come and see," said Donald, who really was quite curious.

Hand in hand, they tiptoed down the passage to Daisy's room. Slowly, shivering a little, Donald pushed open the door.

There was a strange, soft sound in the room.

"Why, it's crying!" cried Daisy. "It must be a lady ghost!"

And indeed it was! The ghost sat on the edge of the bed, sobbing as if her heart was breaking.

Suddenly Donald felt much braver. He walked up to the ghost and touched her on the shoulder. At least, he meant to touch her on the shoulder but his hand went right through it!

"What's the matter?" cried Donald. "Why are you crying?"

"Oh, I'm so unhappy," sobbed the ghost.

"But why?" asked Daisy, handing her a handkerchief. "I always thought ghosts *liked* frightening people."

"Oh, I don't mind *that*," said the ghost, as she wiped away her tears. "But I'm so lonely. Night after night, year after year, floating up and down these passages, with no one to talk to. It's very miserable."

"I can understand that," said Daisy.

"I'd *hate* to stay in this gloomy castle by myself."

Donald thought carefully. "Can't you go and look for another ghost?" he asked. "There must be more around here."

"I haven't got time," said the ghost. "You see, I can only come out after midnight, and this castle is miles from anywhere. I could never go out and be back by dawn."

"We'll see what we can do to help you," said Donald. "I think you ought to let Daisy get some sleep now and come back again tomorrow."

The ghost floated up at once. She was really very polite. She smiled at Daisy. At least she *tried* to smile, but ghosts are not very good at it, and then she sort of glided through the wall.

The next morning, after breakfast, Donald spoke to the hotel manager. "Tell me, my good man," he said, "Are there any ghosts around here?"

The manager looked very serious. "You won't find a ghost *here*, sir," he said. "This is a very *respectable* hotel, but they do say that the old Abbey is haunted."

Just after midnight, Donald and Daisy drove out to the old Abbey.

"Oh, it looks so spooky!" said Daisy, shivering. Just then an owl hooted and Donald nearly jumped out of his skin. They got out of the car and walked into the ruins. There was a full moon and they could see quite clearly, but there was no sign of a ghost.

"Is anyone there?" called Donald bravely.

Suddenly Daisy felt something flapping near her head. "OOOO!" she cried.

"Don't go away, Mr. Ghost!" cried Donald. "We're friends. We only want to talk to you."

All of a sudden they could see a yellowish light shining on some stones ahead of them, and there was the ghost! Quickly Donald told him about the lady ghost in the hotel. "It's a much nicer place," he added, "Quite warm and comfortable. Much nicer than this old ruined abbey. Why don't you come and see?"

The ghost agreed. So they drove back to the hotel, the ghost sitting nervously in the back seat. But he was very pleased to meet the ghost who was waiting in Daisy's bedroom, and she was pleased, too. "Oh, how nice!" she said, flapping her arms. "Now I'll have company in the dark nights and never be lonely again."

Daisy smiled happily. "If only that manager knew!" cried Donald naughtily. "Now he's got *two* ghosts!"

Tiggers Don't Climb Trees

ONE FINE MORNING Kanga had a lot of housework to do, so she sent Roo and Tigger off to have a picnic lunch in the forest.

As they walked along, Tigger told Roo all about the things that Tiggers could do.

"Can they fly?" asked Roo.

"Yes," said Tigger, "they're very good flyers."

"Ohh!" said Roo. "Can they fly as well as Owl?"

"Yes," said Tigger. "Only they don't want to. They just don't like it, somehow."

Roo couldn't understand this, because he thought it would be lovely to be able to fly; but Tigger said it was difficult to explain to anybody who wasn't a Tigger himself.

"Can they jump as far as Kangas?" asked Roo.

"Yes," said Tigger. "When they want to."

"I _love_ jumping," said Roo. "Let's see who can jump farthest, you or me."

"I can," said Tigger. "But we mustn't stop now, or we shall be late."

"Late for what?" asked Roo.

"For whatever we want to be in time for," said Tigger, hurrying on.

In a little while they came to the Pine Trees.

"I can swim," said Roo. "Can Tiggers swim?"

"Of course they can," said Tigger. "They can do everything."

"Can they climb trees better than Winnie-the-Pooh?" asked Roo, stopping under the tallest Pine Tree and looking up at it.

"Climbing trees is what they do best," said Tigger.

"Could they climb this one?"

"They're always climbing trees like that," said Tigger. "Up and down, all day."

"Oo, Tigger, are they really?"

"I'll show you," said Tigger bravely,

"and you can sit on my back and watch me."

So Roo sat on Tigger's back and up they went. And for the first ten feet Tigger said happily, "Up we go!" And for the next ten feet he said, "I always *said* Tiggers could climb trees." And for the next ten feet he said, "Not that it's easy, mind you." And for the next ten feet he said, "Of course, there's the coming-down, too. Backwards. Which will be difficult unless one fell, when it would be . . . EASY!"

And at the word "easy" the branch he was standing on broke suddenly, and he just managed to clutch at the one above him as he felt himself going . . . and then slowly he got his chin over it . . . and then one back paw . . . and then the other . . . until at last he was sitting on it, breathing very quickly, and wishing he had gone swimming instead.

Roo climbed off, and sat down next to him.

"Oo, Tigger," he said, excitedly. "Are we at the top?"

"No," said Tigger.

"Are we going to the top?"

"*No*," said Tigger.

Roo was silent for a little while, and then he said, "Shall we eat our sandwiches, Tigger?" And Tigger said, "Yes, where are they?" And Roo said, "At the bottom of the tree." And Tigger said, "I don't think we'd better eat them just yet." So they didn't.

By and by Winnie-the-Pooh and Piglet came along.

"Look, Pooh!" said Piglet suddenly. "There's something in one of the Pine Trees."

"So there is!" said Pooh, looking up wonderingly. "There's an animal. Why, I do believe it's Tigger and Roo!"

"Hallo, Roo!" called Piglet. "What are you doing?"

"We can't get down, we can't get down!" cried Roo. "Isn't it fun? Tigger and I are living in a tree, like Owl, and we're going to stay here for ever and ever."

"How did you get there, Roo?" asked Piglet.

"On Tigger's back! And Tigger can't climb downwards, because their tails get in the way, only upwards, and Tigger forgot all about that when we started and he's only just remembered. So we've got to stay here for ever and ever."

"Piglet," said Pooh solemnly. "What shall we do?" And in a thoughtful way he began to eat Tigger's and Roo's sandwiches.

Suddenly there was a crackling in the bracken, and Christopher Robin and Eeyore came strolling along together. Winnie-the-Pooh and Piglet hurried up to them.

"Oh, Christopher Robin," cried Pooh, "Tigger and Roo are right up the Pine Tree and they can't get down."

Christopher Robin thought carefully. "I've got an idea!" he cried suddenly. "I'll take off my jacket and we'll each hold a corner, and then Roo and Tigger

can jump into it, and it will be all soft and bouncy for them, and they won't hurt themselves."

When Roo understood what he had to do, he was wildly excited. He squeaked out, "I'm coming!" and jumped—straight into the middle of the jacket. He bounced up almost as high as he was before—and went on bouncing until at last he stopped and said, "Oo, lovely!" and they put him on the ground.

"Come on, Tigger," he called out. "It's easy."

"Come along," called Christopher Robin. "You'll be all right."

But Tigger was very nervous.

"Come on, it's easy!" squeaked Roo. Suddenly Tigger found how easy it was.

"Ow!" he shouted as the tree flew past him.

"Look out!" cried Christopher Robin to the others.

There was a crash, and a tearing noise, and a mixed-up heap of everybody on the ground.

Christopher Robin and Pooh and Piglet picked themselves up first, and then they picked Tigger up. Underneath everybody else was Eeyore.

"Oh, Eeyore!" cried Christopher Robin. "Are you hurt?" And he felt him rather anxiously, and dusted him and helped him to stand up.

But Eeyore only grunted and looked crossly at Tigger who was just as bouncy as ever.

"It's obvious that Tiggers *cannot* climb trees," he said snootily. Then, tossing back his head, he walked off proudly through the forest.

Pinocchio's Adventure at The Puppet Theatre

ONE DAY PINOCCHIO, the little wooden puppet with the long nose, was on his way to school.

He was surprised to hear music floating on the air. It seemed to be coming from a gaily coloured tent that stood in a field near the road. Many people were standing around the tent listening to the music.

Pinocchio was very curious. He wandered over to the tent to see what was happening.

On the tent was a big notice which said "PUPPET THEATRE".

"Oh, how interesting," said Pinocchio to himself. "I've never seen another puppet. I'd love to go in."

But it cost fourpence and Pinocchio didn't have any money. But he did have a new schoolbook which Gepetto the old toymaker had given him.

"Would you like to buy this brand-new book, for four pence?" he asked a man who was standing near him.

The man was a shopkeeper and he agreed, for the book was a bargain at that low price. He would be able to sell it again in his shop.

So Pinocchio took the four pence from the man, bought a ticket and went into the theatre.

It was quite dark inside, but the stage was brightly lit and on it two puppets were dancing. They were called Harlequin and Pulcinello. They were very clever puppets. They sang and told jokes and all the people who were watching laughed and laughed.

Suddenly Harlequin stopped in the

middle of a song and pointed at a seat in the audience.

"Look, Pulcinello!" he cried. "There's another little puppet sitting there."

"Why, so there is!" said Pulcinello excitedly, peering over the footlights. "Come and meet your wooden brothers!"

So Pinocchio jumped on to the stage and the puppets lifted him on to their shoulders and carried him around. They were so happy to see Pinocchio that they quite forgot about going on with the play.

The owner of the theatre was very angry. He was an ugly, fierce-looking man with a bushy black beard. He carried a long, long whip made of wolves' tails all plaited together.

"Get on with the play," he yelled, cracking his whip. Pulcinello and Harlequin were very frightened. They dropped Pinocchio and the man picked him up and hung him on a hook.

When the play was finished, the horrible man told Pulcinello and Harlequin to put Pinocchio on the fire. "I haven't got any wood," he said, "and he'll burn nicely to cook my supper."

Harlequin and Pulcinello were very sad but they had to do what the owner said. If they didn't he would whip them. They picked up poor Pinocchio, who struggled desperately. He kicked his little wooden legs and screamed, "Papa, help me! Help me!" But, of course, Gepetto was far away and couldn't hear him.

Pinocchio cried so much that the man was sorry for him. "All right," he said "I'll burn Harlequin instead."

But Pinocchio didn't like that either. He went down on his knees in front of the fierce man and pleaded, "Please don't hurt Harlequin. Burn me instead!"

The man was astonished. He had never seen such courage before. "What an unusual puppet you are," he said.

"It's very brave of you to try to save me," said Harlequin.

"It's the noblest thing I've ever seen," said Pulcinello.

The old man was really very touched. "All right," he grunted, "I'll just have to eat my supper half-cooked tonight!"

The three puppets were so happy that they held hands and danced round and round.

"I've got to go to school now," said Pinocchio, "but can I come and see you again?"

"Come this evening," said the old man. "You can act in the play with Pulcinello and Harlequin."

Pinocchio clapped his little wooden hands with excitement. "Oh, how lovely! I shall be an actor! My Papa can come and see me, too."

"Here's a ticket for him," said the old man. "I'll find a nice song for you to sing. Come early so that you can practise it."

What a wonderful evening they all had! Everyone loved the play. And Gepetto, the old toymaker, was very, very proud of his little wooden puppet, Pinocchio.

The Silly Chicken

THE CUNNING old fox had tried many times to catch the turkeys and chickens living in the chicken-coop. But he had never been successful. The trouble was there was a tall fence around the yard; although the fox had tried and tried, he just couldn't climb over it.

"I must get the chickens and turkeys to come out of the yard," he said to himself. "Then I must get them into my den."

He thought and thought until at last he had a plan.

Now, in the yard there was one chicken who looked very stupid. This little chicken spent all day playing with a yoyo.

One day the fox crept to the fence and peered over it. There was the chicken, playing with his yoyo as usual.

Suddenly the fox threw a big wooden star at the chicken's head and at the same time he banged the fence making a terrible noise.

The chicken was quite stunned. He looked at the star that had hit him, heard the frightful noise and cried, "The sky's falling down! The sky's falling down!"

The fox nearly died with laughter.

All the inhabitants of the chicken-coop rushed into the yard, squawking madly.

"Oh, where shall we hide? Where shall we hide!" they cried. "The sky is falling down!"

"We'd better get outside," said a big fat cockerel, who was the chief of the chicken-coop.

"There's a cave nearby," said a little red hen. "We'll be safe there."

Well, this cave was really the fox's den.

One by one the chickens and the turkeys marched into the cave. As soon as they were all inside, the wicked old fox slammed the door. He had caught them all!

"Well, my beauties, quite a little banquet!" he cried, licking his lips. "Who's going to be first for the pot?"

But suddenly the little chicken took his yoyo and aimed it with all his might at the fox's head.

The fox gave a big groan and fell to the ground.

"Quick!" cried the little chicken. "Get out all of you! As fast as you can!"

One by one the turkeys and chickens rushed through the door. The fox was so stunned and dizzy that he just couldn't stop them.

At last they were all outside. Quickly they made their way back to the chicken-coop.

The little chicken was the hero of the day. How proud he felt!

But the poor fox only felt very, very disappointed.

The silly little chicken wasn't so silly after all, was he?

The Poor Little Pig

PINKERTON WAS THE TINIEST of eight little pigs who had just been born on the farm.

Poor little Pinkerton was feeling very sad. Every day, when it was time to eat, his brothers would all push him to one side so that he could not get any milk from his mother. Not even a teeny-weeny bit.

Poor Pinkerton was starving.

"Things can't go on like this," he sobbed to himself. "I'll have to try to find some food somewhere else."

So he left his mother and brothers and trotted around the farm looking for something nice to eat.

But oh dear! although he looked and looked, he couldn't find a thing!

He tried to eat some of the hen's corn but she was very angry and chased after him, flapping her wings furiously. "Get away, you cheeky little pig!" she squawked. She was afraid that Pinkerton would hurt her little chickens.

Then the little pig thought that perhaps the cow would give him some of *her* milk. But the cow kicked her legs at him angrily.

"Go away, you silly little pig!" she mooed. "I need my milk for my own calf."

Quickly Pinkerton ran away across the yard. There he saw the granary, full of lovely corn.

"I'll go and eat some of that," he said to himself. He was just going in the door when he heard a loud "Wouff! Wouff!"

"Where do you think you're going?" said an angry voice. It was the watchdog! "Get out of here at once." And the dog barked so loudly and furiously that the poor little pig was very, very frightened.

By this time Pinkerton was very tired. So he sat down to rest in a quiet corner away from all the animals. To his great surprise, he saw a saucer of milk on the ground. How delicious it looked.

"Ooo, I'll just have a sip of that," he said to himself, and was just about to drink the milk when he heard a loud "Miaow!" behind him. It was the cat.

"How dare you touch my milk!" snarled the cat. "Go away at once, before I scratch you!"

Poor Pinkerton ran away as fast as his little legs could carry him.

"Oh dear! Oh dear!" he sobbed. "Nobody loves me. I shall die of hunger!"

Suddenly he heard a gentle voice at his side. It was his mother!

"Pinkerton! Where have you been?" she said softly. "I've been looking for you everywhere! I know your naughty brothers push you away so I've kept some milk just for you."

How happy Pinkerton was to see his mother! And what a lovely feed he had!

Every day his mother gave him some milk all by himself and soon he was so strong that *he* was able to push his brothers away!

The Chilly Penguin

LITTLE PAUL was not like other penguins. In fact, he was a very *strange* little penguin. All the other penguins liked the life they led. They enjoyed skiing, skating on the ice and making beautiful snowmen, but Little Paul seldom went out. He stayed at home, crouched over the stove, trying to keep warm. For Little Paul was a very chilly penguin, so chilly, indeed, that he couldn't bear to go outside in the snow.

On the walls of his igloo hung many pictures of the South Seas. Little Paul loved to look at their bright colours and their golden beaches and waving palm trees. "How I wish I could go there!" he sighed. "How wonderful it would be to lie in the sun and feel warm . . . really warm!"

One day, when he was feeling particularly cold, he made up his mind. "I'm emigrating to Hawaii," he said to his friends. The other penguins looked at him in astonishment. They thought he'd gone mad.

Little Paul cut a block of ice from his house with a large saw. Then he made it into the shape of a boat. He put up the mast, and a sail, and soon was ready to start his great adventure.

Waving gaily to his friends who had come to see him off, he set course for South America.

As he sailed along, Little Paul had many adventures. Day by day he felt less cold, but he wanted to feel really hot. He wanted to be so hot that he would start sweating!

So on and on he sailed. But one day a terrible thing happened. It was now so hot that his little boat began to melt! First one side melted, then another, until there was only a little bit left, on which stood the mast and sail.

Soon that melted, too, and Little Paul fell plop! plop! into the water.

Fortunately he was a very good swim-mer and luckily he was just passing a tropical island.

At once Little Paul made for the island and soon he was wading on to the golden sands. He looked around him at the graceful palm-trees and sighed with satisfaction. It was just like one of the pictures he had at home. It was just the place he was looking for!

Little Paul quickly made himself at home. All the animals welcomed him, even though they had never seen such a strange-looking creature before.

Little Paul was soon living comfortably. Every day he swam in the warm blue sea, and he lay in his hammock sipping the icy-cool drinks that his turtle-servant brought him. He didn't mind the heat at all. In fact, he loved it.

Wasn't he a strange fellow?

If you ever go to a tropical island and see a penguin lying in the sun, then you'll know it's Little Paul because he's the only penguin in the whole world who likes feeling hot!

Peter Pan's Victory

CAPTAIN HOOK, the ferocious leader of the pirates, was feeling very angry. Every time he fought with Peter Pan, he never managed to win a single battle. How could he win when the boy kept on flying round him? It wasn't fair!

One day Captain Hook said slyly to Peter Pan, "I wonder if you're brave enough to fight with me without flying?"

"Of course I am!" replied Peter Pan. "I'll show you that I can beat you even though my feet won't leave the ground."

Now, the wicked Captain Hook told his pirates that as soon as they had a chance they were to catch Peter Pan. It should be easy because he had promised not to fly. But Peter Pan was really much cleverer than Captain Hook thought. He knew that his old enemy was not to be trusted and that he would make some wicked plan. So he told Tinker Bell to spread some of her magic golden dust over Captain Hook. Now, it was because of this magic dust that Peter was able to fly—now Captain Hook would be able to fly, too!

Drawing his gleaming sword, Captain Hook ran at Peter. He was just about to dash his sword at the boy when, to his astonishment, he found he was flying through the air! Screaming with rage, Captain Hook flew from side to side of

the boat. Below him, Peter Pan stood—laughing his head off!

At last, Captain Hook managed to get back on to the deck. "I'll get you for that!" he cried in a terrible voice. Once more he charged Peter with his sword, but once more his feet left the deck! Up, up he flew banging himself hard against the mast of the ship.

Down he fell. Bump! Right on top of the pirates who were waiting to catch the brave young man. They all crashed in a heap to the deck, and then slid into the sea.

Peter laughed so much that his sides ached. He rushed to the side of the ship and looked at all the heads bobbing in the water.

"You see, Captain Hook," he cried. "I can beat you even when I don't fly!"

But the wicked pirate did not answer.

He was too busy trying to swim to the bank before a crocodile reached him.

Because Captain Hook *hated* crocodiles. But that's another story . . .

Dumbo Learns to Fly

AN EXCITING THING had just happened.

The train in which the Circus was travelling had just been visited by the Stork. A little elephant had been born. His mother was surprised to see that her new baby had very large ears, but she was so pleased that he had arrived that she did not mind this at all.

When the Circus arrived in the city, the Big Top was set up in a large field on the outskirts. The next day the circus animals and artists marched through the city so that the people could see them. The band played and the crowd waved. What an exciting parade it was! Little

Dumbo marched, too, by the side of his mother. But he felt very sad because when the people saw his big ears they pointed at him rudely and laughed and laughed.

Dumbo liked it in the Circus. His mother looked after him well. She bathed him every day, in his own special bath tub, and gave him nice food to eat. "You're a beautiful little elephant," she said. "It doesn't matter what other people say. You mustn't care about them."

One day some naughty boys came to the Circus and made fun of Dumbo. His mother was very angry. She charged at

the boys and kicked them. The Ringmaster was very cross. He ordered her to be chained to a post as a punishment for losing her temper.

Poor Dumbo was very unhappy to see his mother tied up. Little Timothy Mouse took pity on him and tried to cheer him up.

"Let's go for a little walk in the country," he said to Dumbo.

So off they went together. It was quite a long walk to the country and they both got very tired.

"Let's rest under this tree for a while," said Timothy Mouse.

So they both sat down and leaned against the trunk of the tree. Soon they were fast asleep.

When Timothy Mouse woke up, it was almost dark. To his astonishment he saw that he and Dumbo were now sitting on a branch at the very *top* of the tree!

"How on earth did we get here?" asked Timothy.

"The little elephant *flew* up," said a bird who was sitting on a branch nearby.

"Yes," said some others excitedly. "He put you on his trunk and he *flew* up. Just like one of us."

Timothy Mouse could hardly believe it. As soon as they reached the Circus again, Timothy told the Ringmaster.

Now, an elephant who can *fly* is a very rare thing. In fact, it's never been heard of before. When he heard the news, the Ringmaster freed Dumbo's mother at once and a big, fat contract was drawn up.

Dumbo became the Star of the Circus. *Everybody* came to see him fly high above the ring. What a wonderful sight it was!

No one ever laughed at Dumbo, the flying elephant, again.

Morris The Midget Moose

OF ALL THE MOOSE in the herd, Morris was the most handsome. His skin was the shiniest, his eyes the brightest, and his antlers were the biggest of all. They were, in fact, much much bigger than those of other animals.

But there was one thing wrong with him. He was very small. He was so small, indeed, that he was almost a midget moose.

He tried to fight the other moose, but they were much too big and the only thing he could do was run between their legs like a little galloping puff of wind!

All the other moose made fun of him and he was so unhappy that, one day, he ran away from the herd. "I'd rather live alone," he said to himself, "than stay with those silly *big* moose."

One afternoon Morris was grazing by the bank of a little stream when he saw another moose looking at him from across the water. The moose was the tallest and biggest Morris had ever seen. He was much taller than the moose in the herd, but there was one thing wrong with him.

His antlers were so small that they could hardly be seen at all!

This moose was called Barnaby and he and Morris soon became good friends.

One day, while he was grazing on the hillside with Barnaby, Morris suddenly said, "What a pity you don't have big antlers like mine. You would be so fierce then."

"Yes," said Barnaby, "and what a pity you aren't tall and big like me. *You* would be so strong then."

The two creatures looked at each other and they both had the same idea at the same time.

"'That's it!" they cried. "Together we make a perfect moose. The most magnificent moose in the whole world!"

"I'll get on your back," said Morris.

"So that your antlers will be *my* antlers!" cried Barnaby.

"And your strong body will be *my* strong body!" cried Morris.

So Morris climbed on to Barnaby's back. Together they formed the most powerful and mighty moose that's ever been seen!

Between the two of them, they looked so fierce that no one dared to make fun of them. The moose, in fact, decided to make them the leader of the herd.

Together, Morris and Barnaby made the strongest leader that the moose had ever had.

But they were also the strangest, don't you think?

Pecos Bill The Cowboy

I EXPECT YOU'VE HEARD of Pecos Bill. He was the bravest cowboy in the West.

Here is a picture of him on his horse.

His horse was famous, too. He was a lovely chestnut and his name was Whirlwind. Look at them charging over the prairie . . .

Pecos Bill was such a wonderful rider. He and Whirlwind rode over the range together from end to end . . . through deep ravines . . . across flooded rivers . . . up steep canyons. Because of his brave deeds, *everyone* knew Pecos Bill. And everybody talked about him.

If anyone was in trouble, they always sent for Pecos Bill. If an outlaw was frightening anyone, Pecos Bill came riding out to capture him. If the Sheriff needed help, he called for Pecos Bill, because Pecos Bill wasn't afraid of anyone.

Pecos Bill had many exciting adventures and he caught many wicked bandits. All bad men were afraid of him and all honest people admired him . . . because Pecos Bill was the fastest shot in the West. And he never missed.

Pecos Bill could be a good friend but a deadly enemy.

Would *you* like to have met him?

Peter And The Wolf

PETER WAS A LITTLE BOY who lived far away in Russia. Like all little boys, Peter loved adventure. And he loved to play games. He had a gun which fired corks and he often pretended to hunt wolves with it.

There was one particular wolf who was making a great nuisance of himself in the district. Everyone was afraid of him.

One day, when Peter looked out of the window, what do you think he saw?

There was his friend the cat sitting on one branch of a tree, there was his friend the woodpecker sitting on another, and underneath, prowling round and round the tree and growling horribly, was the huge, grey, savage wolf!

Suddenly Peter had a clever idea. He got the long coil of strong rope that Grandfather kept in the cupboard and rushed outside. He climbed on to the top of the garden wall, then grabbed a branch of the tree and carefully climbed into it.

He whispered to the bird, "Fly around the wolf's head. Drive him crazy!"

The little bird flew down at once, straight at the wolf. "Grrr! Grrr!" the wolf snapped wildly.

Meanwhile, Peter tied one end of the rope into a lassoo. He twirled it and dropped it carefully over the wolf's big, bushy tail, and pulled it tight. Then he pulled the wolf up into the tree. The wolf snarled and growled, and yelped and howled, but he just couldn't get free.

How surprised the huntsmen were when they came riding by. "What a clever boy!" they cried.

Peter was very proud. And so was Grandfather.

Tromper The Hero

TROMPER, THE LITTLE ELEPHANT, ran happily along, carrying a huge bunch of flowers in his trunk. It was Stripey's birthday and he had been invited to her party.

When he arrived, he found his other friends already there. There was Hiram, the hippopotamus, Kim, the little bear, and Joey, the naughtiest monkey in the whole forest.

"When we've eaten all the cake we'll go and play in the little tree-house," said Stripey.

Just then the fat old hippopotamus did a silly thing. He blew out the candles on Stripey's cake so hard that all the top of the cake flew into Tromper's face.

How everyone laughed! Poor Tromper's face was covered with chocolate!

Tromper burst into tears. "How unkind you are to make fun of me," he said with a sob. "I shall go away!"

So poor Tromper went off by himself.

As he was sitting sadly underneath a coconut tree, he suddenly heard a loud cry of alarm. And another! And another!

"The tree house is on fire! The tree-house is on fire! Help! Help!"

At once Tromper rushed down to the

river and filled his trunk with water. Then he called the tallest giraffe in the forest. Tromper climbed up the giraffe's long neck and held on tightly. The giraffe galloped off to the tree-house . . .

What a sight it was! Smoke was rising from it in a great cloud and Stripey, Kim and Joey looked out with very frightened faces.

"Don't worry!" cried Tromper. "We'll soon have the fire out!"

He squirted the water in his trunk over the flames. They sizzled and spluttered and soon they were all out. Then, one at a time, Tromper lifted his friends down from the tree-house.

Stripey came first. Tromper curled his trunk around her and lifted her gently out of the tree-house. Then giraffe bent his long neck and Tromper put Stripey

safely on the ground under the tree.

"Oh, thank you, thank you, Tromper," she purred happily. "You were just in time."

Then Tromper lifted down the little bear and the monkey.

The fat old hippopotamus stood by watching them. He went up to Tromper and said, "I am sorry I was so rude, Tromper. You've done a brave thing to-day."

"Yes," said Stripey. "A clever thing, too. You must forgive us, Tromper. We'll never laugh at you again."

Tromper felt so happy.

"There are still some cakes and jellies left," said Stripey. "Let's go on with the party."

So they did. And Giraffe joined in, too. What a lovely time they all had!

The Sad Little Car

WHEN JOHNNY SAW the little blue car in the window of the car showroom he was sure that it was just the car he wanted.

At once he went into the showroom and bought it.

He was very pleased with it. The little blue car rode so well. Johnny loved going out on the motorway. The little blue car loved it, too, and his little engine throbbed softly and happily.

Johnny and the little blue car had lots of good times together. Johnny loved his car and the little blue car loved his master, because Johnny treated him well. He always washed the dust and dirt off and then polished him so that his bodywork shone like glass.

The little blue car stayed with Johnny for a long time. But one day he felt very ill. Johnny took him to a car-doctor. The car-doctor (who was really a mechanic) looked at the little car carefully . . . all over.

"He needs a few spare parts," said the car-doctor to Johnny. "But I'm afraid he won't be quite the same again. He is getting a bit old, you know."

So Johnny sold the little blue car. The little blue car stood sadly in the corner of the dealer's yard. "Nobody wants me," he said to himself sadly. But he was wrong. One day a man came and bought him.

His now owner didn't treat him very well, however. The little blue car was left to sleep in the street in all kinds of weather. Sometimes he was covered with snow and then he shivered with cold.

Sometimes the sun shone on him so strongly that all his bodywork was cracked.

The poor little blue car was very unhappy. At last the day came when he could go no further. He stopped suddenly in the street and he just couldn't get started again.

The little blue car was towed away to a junk-yard.

"This is really the end," sighed the little blue car.

But one evening a young man happened to pass by the junk-yard. He saw the little blue car and stopped. Then he walked over to the little blue car and looked at him carefully. There was a very pleased look on his face and his eyes were kind.

The little blue car liked the look of the young man. "Please buy me," he whispered to himself.

It was as if the young man had heard him, for at once he made up his mind. "I'll take it!" he said.

The little blue car rode to the young man's house as best as he could, although he wasn't feeling very well. But he soon began to feel better. The young man put him in a shed and spent days and days working on him. He cleaned his engine, put in some nice new parts, gave him some new tyres, cleaned his windows and painted and polished him until he shone like glass again.

The little blue car looked as good as the day when he had first stood in the showroom. How happy he was!

Eeyore Loses His Tail

"I CAN'T FIND IT!" said Eeyore sadly one day, searching everywhere.

"What have you lost?" asked Christopher Robin.

"My tail," said Eeyore, neighing unhappily. "I had it yesterday when I walked in the wood, but when I woke up this morning it was gone."

Christopher helped him to look for it. He walked through the wood searching on all sides, but there was no sign of it.

"I'll go and ask Owl," said Christopher Robin. "He's very wise. He's sure to know where it is."

Christopher Robin walked to the big oak tree where Owl lived. He pulled the rope of Owl's bell and waited.

Soon Owl appeared, blinking his eyes in the sunlight. "Can't a fellow get some sleep?" he said crossly. Then he saw Christopher Robin. "Oh, it's you," he said. "What can I do for you?"

"It's Eeyore's tail," said Christopher Robin. "The silly donkey's gone and lost it. Have you seen it by any chance?"

The Owl scratched his head. "I'm afraid not," he said. Just then, Christopher Robin noticed the bell-rope he had just pulled. "That's a funny looking bell-rope," he said in a puzzled voice.

"Isn't it smart?" said Owl. "I found it yesterday, hanging over a bush."

Christopher Robin sighed. "I'm afraid I'll have to take it," he said. "It's Eeyore's tail."

Christopher Robin tried to fix the tail on as best he could. "Don't lose it again," he said.

Journey Into Space

DONALD HAS MADE a space ship and is thinking of going to the moon.

His little nephews, Huey, Dewey and Louie, want to go with him on this great adventure. And Donald has agreed.

At last everything is ready.

All four of them climb aboard, wearing their special brightly coloured space-suits.

Wouldn't *you* like to go with them?

There is a great bang like thunder. Then a great crackle as the space-ship's fuel begins to burn.

BLAST OFF! The space-ship shakes from side to side. Slowly . . . it begins to lift off. Up . . . up it rises, faster and faster, like a great red arrow into the sky. WHOOSH!

Soon the earth is far away, a tiny grey ball in space.

"Goodbye, earth!" cried Donald.

"Moon, here we come!" yelled Huey, Dewey and Louie.

Now the rocket separated from the space-ship. The four brave astronauts are speeding towards the moon. How excited they are. It really is a wonderful adventure.

For days and days they speed through space until, at last, they see the rocky surface of the moon below them.

"Prepare for landing!" cries Donald. They are almost there . . .

They should have landed by now. Do you think Donald and his three little nephews are *still* on the moon?

Manni Looks For Adventure

MANNI, THE LITTLE DONKEY, was feeling very bored. Life was very dull on the farm and he wished something exciting would happen.

"I'm going to the wood to look for adventure," he said one day.

"No, don't do that, little donkey," neighed the horses. "Something may happen to you. It's better for you to stay here. There is danger in the wood."

"Yes, little donkey," quacked the ducks. "It's safe in the farmyard. You shouldn't go outside."

But Manni's mind was made up. One morning the farmer left the gate open and Manni trotted through it. He was off to look for adventure!

Soon he reached the wood. There he met a squirrel with a big bushy tail and they became good friends.

"Is it possible to find adventure in this wood?" Manni asked him.

"Yes indeed!" said the little squirrel. "The red fox lives here and he is very wicked."

Manni pricked up his ears. "I'm not

afraid," he said bravely. "I would like to see him."

"You wouldn't say that if you knew him," said the squirrel wisely. "You should go back to the farm, then you wouldn't be in danger of meeting him."

Manni met many animals in the wood and they all said the same thing.

"He's very cunning," said the deer.

"He's very strong," said the rabbits.

"You can't trust him," said the birds.

"Are you talking about *me*, by any chance?" said a sly voice.

All the animals looked around in fear. It was the fox! He stood by the side of the path, smiling wickedly and showing all his big, sharp teeth.

All the animals turned and ran as fast as they could. But Manni did not move.

Suddenly Manni lifted his head and brayed so loudly that the whole wood shook from end to end.

The fox was terrified. He had never heard such a terrible noise before!

He put up his paws to cover his ears and then jumped into the bushes, running off as fast as his legs could carry him.

And do you know? He never came back to that wood again.

All the animals of the wood were so grateful to Manni for getting rid of their fierce enemy. Manni was happy, too, for he had found an adventure.

All the animals walked with him back to the farm, and said goodbye to him at the gate.

"You must come and see us often," said the deer, and the rabbits and the birds.

And sometimes, when Manni felt bored, he used to trot down the road and go to have a chat with his friends in the wood.

He *still* liked looking for adventure!

Bongo Runs Away

LOOK AT THIS PICTURE of Bongo, the little bear.

Bongo is the Star of the Circus. He is the famous high-wire artist. He balances on his little one-wheeled bicycle and rides on the wire high above the crowd. How the people love him!

Bongo is a great artist, but to tell the truth he is often very sad. Although he *likes* the applause of the crowd—you can see him bowing in the picture—it doesn't make up for the fact that he is a prisoner. When the show is over, he is put back into his cage and the door is locked. How he longs to go outside and see the world.

One night his keeper forgot to lock his cage when he brought him his supper. Bongo waited until it was dark and everyone was asleep. Carrying his little bicycle, he crept out of his cage and quietly tiptoed past the silent tents and caravans of the Circus. No one saw him.

As soon as he reached the gate, he got on his bicycle and cycled as fast as he could into the country.

Now Bongo is very happy. For the first time in his life he is tasting the delights of freedom. He cycles in the sunshine all over the country, seeing all the beautiful things he had never seen before.

Now Bongo is his own master. He can go where he likes and do what he likes.

A Cure for Sneezers

I'M SURE THAT very few of you like medicine.

Most children *hate* it.

You know the dwarfs who live with Snow-White? Well . . . at one time they used to hate it, too. But now they take it without making a fuss. Even the nastiest sort of medicine, and this is why . . .

It happened during the long cold winter. One after another, the dwarfs caught a terrible cold. How miserable they were! They went around the little cottage, coughing and sneezing miserably. Some of them felt so bad that they had to go to bed.

Doc, who was the wisest one, told them that they must take some medicine if they wanted to get better quickly. Off he went to the village to get some. When he returned, all the dwarfs crowded around him and Doc took out the bottle. Inside was a thick yellow syrup. Doc took out the cork and poured some into a spoon. The first dwarf, Happy, took a sip.

"Ugh! It's awful!" he cried, making a terrible face.

"Yes," said Doc sternly, "but it's good for you."

One after another, the dwarfs bravely took their medicine.

All except one.

He refused absolutely.

Do you know who it was?   . .

All the dwarfs soon got better, but the one who would not take his medicine never really got better at all.

His cold is gone but he still sneezes all the time.

Yes! His name is Sneezy.

Did you guess?

Adventure At The Pole

ONE DAY, PEDRO, the South American parrot, invited his friends Donald and Goofy to take a trip with him in the aeroplane which he had bought.

So one fine day off they flew into the wide blue sky.

However, Pedro didn't know how to navigate very well and soon they were lost! All around them were thick, white clouds. On and on they flew, and when the clouds disappeared, to their astonishment, they found they were flying over the South Pole!

To make matters worse, they were almost out of fuel. There was only one thing to do. They would have to land.

Pedro brought the plane down safely near a colony of penguins who all rushed out to greet them. They were very friendly and helpful to the travellers.

The penguins gave them some fuel which they had taken a long time ago from an abandoned boat, and they showed them the route they must take in order to arrive back in South America.

Our friends wanted to thank the penguins, so they unpacked the food which they had in the plane and they all had a wonderful feast.

What a wonderful party they had! All night they danced merrily on the ice and sang and ate. In the morning Pedro, Donald and Goofy boarded the plane, and, taking the right course this time, soon they were flying home.

"We were really very lucky," said Pedro. "How kind the penguins were to help us."

Little Hiawatha

LITTLE HIAWATHA's father had forbidden him to fish in the big river because it was too dangerous.

But one day Hiawatha got out his little canoe and sailed down to the big river.

It was spring-time and high tide so there was a lot of water in the river. The river swirled dangerously.

Suddenly, to his horror, Hiawatha found that he had been caught by the strong current!

There was nothing he could do! It was impossible to use the paddles. The current swept the boat on, and Little Hiawatha clung frightened to the sides. The waves became stronger and stronger . . . the fragile boat would soon break . . .

"Help! Help!" cried the terrified Little Hiawatha.

Luckily his father heard him. He ran swiftly along the bank and threw a long rope at the little boat. Hiawatha tried to catch it, but twice the rope fell short and plonked into the water.

On the third try, Little Hiawatha managed to catch it. Quickly he tied it to the little boat.

Little Hiawatha's father now began to pull on the rope. He was a very strong man and slowly but steadily he was able to turn the little boat towards the bank and pull it in.

Little Hiawatha was so glad to step on dry land.

"You foolish boy! said his father angrily. "I shall have to punish you for being so disobedient."

So Little Hiawatha wasn't allowed to go fishing for two whole weeks. It was his own silly fault, wasn't it?

Pluto And The Bees

PLUTO WAS SLEEPING peacefully guarding the beautiful pudding which Mickey had made for tea. Suddenly he gave a sharp yelp. Something had stung him! He looked up angrily.

A large cloud of bees was buzzing around the pudding, trying to eat it. "Get away! Scat!" cried Pluto, flicking his tail angrily at the bees.

But the bees didn't pay the slightest attention to him.

Buzz! Buzz! Buzz! They zoomed down over the pudding. Pluto tried to frighten them with a fierce bark, "Whouff! Whouff!" but the bees would not go away.

Then he tried to hit them with his tail and his paws. But it was useless. Suddenly a huge bee flew straight at Pluto. And can you guess what the bee did?

Zoom! He stung him right on his shiny black nose.

"Aaaaaaw!" cried Pluto in agony. He stepped back and knocked over the table. The pudding came crashing to the ground. Plop!

When Mickey came home and saw his lovely pudding ruined, he thought that Pluto had knocked over the table on purpose in order to eat the pudding.

"Naughty dog!" said Mickey crossly. "You shan't have any pudding for a week!"

Pluto felt very sad. But then Mickey noticed the big red swelling on Pluto's nose and he realised what had happened. "Never mind, Pluto," he said. "You can lick up that pudding, and I'll make a nice new one."

"Wouff! Wouff!" said Pluto happily.

The Greedy Penguin

ONE DAY DONALD received a parcel from his friends at the South Pole.

Eagerly he opened it. What do you think was inside? A penguin! The prettiest penguin he had ever seen! How surprised Donald was!

Donald tried to make him feel at home, but as the days went by he could see that the little penguin wasn't very happy. He sat around miserably and didn't seem to have enough energy even to walk around the house.

"What's wrong?" asked Donald anxiously one day.

"It's so hot," said the little penguin. "How I miss the lovely cold ice and snow of the Pole."

Suddenly Donald had a good idea. He would put the little penguin in the freezer!

The little penguin was very happy in his new home and soon began to feel better. But when Donald opened the freezer in the evening he found that the little penguin had eaten everything that was inside! All the milk and the cream and the butter and the bacon and the sausages and the trifle . . .

"Oh dear!" said Donald, "Now we haven't anything for supper. This is no way for a nice polite little penguin to behave."

The little penguin looked so sad, and jumped down from the freezer with such a comical look on his face, that Donald couldn't blame him any more.

"I suppose you couldn't really help it!" he laughed. "All that nice food was much too tempting. Especially when you've had to look at it all day!"

Mickey Mouse's Birthday

MICKEY WAS FAST ASLEEP in bed when suddenly the telephone rang.

"Who on earth can it be at this early hour?" said Mickey to himself. To his surprise, he heard a mysterious voice say, "Don't leave your house today! It is very important!"

"Why not?" asked Mickey, in a very puzzled voice. "What will happen? This is very strange . . . Who are you?"

But the unknown caller had gone.

Mickey got up, feeling rather worried. He had just finished breakfast when the phone rang again. Once more the strange caller said, "Don't go out today! It is very important!"

The mysterious call was repeated three more times during the morning. The little mouse now felt very frightened indeed.

Suddenly a bell rang again. But this time it was a different bell. It was the front door and not the telephone. Mickey went to open it . . .

What a surprise he had!

There were all his friends, all carrying exciting-looking parcels and packages.

"Happy Birthday, Mickey!" cried Minnie. "You've probably forgotten, but it's your birthday today!"

"Why, so it is," said Mickey. "And *you* were the mysterious caller!"

"Yes," quacked Donald. "We wanted to have a party, so we had to make sure you would stay in!"

"Well, come in," said Mickey, "and let's get started!"

142

The Ball of Wool

FIGARO HAD JUST FOUND a beautiful ball of red wool. And which cat doesn't like playing with such an attractive toy?

At first he hit it gently with his paw. The ball of wool rolled along the floor. Figaro ran after it and hit it again. This time a long thread came out of the ball. Figaro hit the ball again and the long thread wound around his paw.

Figaro loved this new game. Again and again he sent the ball flying. Then he ran after it and pounced on it. More and more threads came out of the ball of wool. They all wound around Figaro and soon he could hardly be seen. He looked like a big fluffy red ball.

Figaro tried to free himself. But it was impossible! His four legs were caught *and* his tail. He was a prisoner! Now he began to feel frightened so he cried out.

"Help! Help! Get me out!" he miaowed.

Pinocchio heard him and came rushing in. "Oh you naughty pussy!" he cried. "You've spoilt all the wool. Now there won't be enough to finish my red waistcoat."

Pinocchio began to untie Figaro. It was very difficult and took a long time. At last Figaro was free. "Miaow! Miaow!" he cried, and began to lick Pinocchio's hand, for he knew he had done a bad thing.

"It's nice to play," said Pinocchio. "But you must only play with things you're allowed to play with. You see what your little game has done?"

"Miaow," said Figaro sadly. He really did feel very sorry.

Apple Tarts For Tea

DONALD'S LITTLE NEPHEWS love their grandmother very much. She loves them, too.

Sometimes, of course, she gets rather cross and she scolds Huey, Dewey and Louie when they are naughty. But at the same time she spoils them and always gives them a present on their birthdays and at Christmas.

Donald's little nephews love going to visit her. Grandmother is a wonderful cook and she always makes lots of nice things for them to eat. When she knows that they are coming, she always makes lots of their favourite cakes—and apple tarts.

Do *you* like apple tart?

I expect you do.

Can you see Grandmother in the picture?

She has just taken the tarts out of the oven. What a lovely tea-party they are going to have!

After tea Huey, Dewey and Louie often go for a walk with Grandmother.

Sometimes they make her angry because they do not cross the road carefully, or they spoil their best shoes by splashing through the puddles.

Donald doesn't like to see Grandmother angry. "You mustn't upset her," he tells his nephews. "Old people don't like to be upset."

"But we don't really mean it," say the nephews. "She knows that we love her very much."

The Monkey Orchestra

MOWGLI WAS WALKING through the jungle one morning, singing a merry song, when he met his good friend Baloo, the Bear.

"What a beautiful song!" he said. "What a pity there isn't any music to accompany you. If there was, it would be perfect."

Suddenly there was a swishing sound in the branches of the tree above them. Baloo and Mowgli looked up. It was the monkeys.

They swung down, howling and shrieking.

The monkeys *always* made a lot of noise.

"We heard you," they chattered. "We will make music for you."

"We would be delighted," said Baloo, "but how can you? You haven't any guitars, or drums, or anything like that."

But the monkeys only laughed. "We don't need any of them," they cried. "Just watch!"

The monkeys bounded over to an old hollow tree trunk that was lying on the ground. They hit it with the palms of their hands and made a most delightful sound.

"What a wonderful touch!" exclaimed Mowgli. "What a marvellous orchestra you make!"

So Mowgli sang his song and the monkey orchestra beat the hollow trunk. The rhythm of the monkeys was so marvellous that Baloo just had to dance and sing, too. "Boopedy-doo! Boopedy-doo!"

What a lovely time they all had!

Wart Fights
The Robber-Giant

THIS IS A STORY about Wart, the adopted son of Sir Ector, the kindly knight, and his half-brother Kay.

Now, Sir Ector wanted his own son Kay to grow up brave, for one day he would become Sir Kay and master of the castle. Now, this elder boy was big and strong but he was also stubborn and rather lazy.

Wart was younger than Kay and very much smaller. But he was a merry little fellow and not a bit jealous of Kay.

One day Sir Ector called his two sons and said to them, "A great robber giant lives in the mountains. In his shield there is a precious jewel. I want you to go and find him and bring back the jewel."

So Kay and Wart set out. They walked for miles and miles, and the road became steeper and rockier, but there was no sign of the robber.

"Oh dear," said Kay yawning. "I'm much too tired to go any farther. I think I'll have a little rest."

So Kay unbuckled his sword and shield and sat down on the rocky ground, leaning his back against a tree. Soon he was fast asleep.

Very quickly Wart picked up Kay's sword and shield. He would look for the giant himself!

He hurried on into the mountains until he came to the huge black mouth of a cave. He felt very frightened but he called out bravely, "Is there anyone there?"

The only answer was a deep rumble like thunder. Suddenly a tall dark shape blacked the entrance to the cave.

"Who dares to wake me up?" roared a terrible voice.

It was the robber giant.

In the middle of his shield Wart saw the huge jewel.

"Stand and fight!" cried Wart bravely, brandishing his sword.

The robber only laughed, and walked towards Wart with huge strides.

But Wart did not move. Holding his shield in front of him, he stood firm.

The robber raised his sword. Just as he was about to strike, Wart darted aside.

The robber giant's sword crashed down to the ground, hitting it with such a powerful stroke that the CLANG echoed from rock to rock.

The robber swore a frightful oath and turned to face Wart. Again he raised his sword for a mighty swing. This time Wart ducked and the robber fell over him, crashing to the ground with a heavy THUD.

At once Wart raised his sword and pierced the robber's chest. The giant was dead!

Wart took the sparkling jewel from the robber's shield and went back to the tree where Kay was lying. He was still asleep. Wart put the jewel into his pocket and did not say anything about his fight.

Wart and Kay went on with their search and soon they came to the cave where they found the dead giant. Kay was sad when he saw that the jewel had gone, but he really was glad that the robber was dead because he had been afraid of fighting him.

So Wart and Kay returned to the castle.

Kay told his father that the wicked giant was dead but that there was no sign of the jewel.

Sir Ector's face was as black as a thundercloud. "Where can it be?" he roared.

Wart opened his hand. There, on his palm, lay the brilliant sparkling jewel.

"Is this what you wanted?" he asked quietly.

Sir Ector could hardly believe his eyes. The jewel flashed as if it were on fire.

Then Wart told Sir Ector how he had fought the robber giant and taken the jewel.

Sir Ector was not very pleased. He had wanted his son, Kay, to succeed and not his scrawny adopted son. But all the nobles and knights were watching. Sir Ector had to put a brave face on it.

"Well done, lad," he said. "You may grow up into a fine strong man yet."

And of course he did. For before he was very much older Wart made the old legend come true. He pulled the sword from the stone and became the great and noble King Arthur of England.

The Lion King Longs For Spots

THE LION KING OF NABOOMBU looked at himself in the mirror and sighed.

"I'm sick of the sight of this old face," he said to himself, tossing back his mane. "It's such a dull brown. I wish I could be *different* for a change."

He looked at his reflection thoughtfully. "Stripes, perhaps," he said. "Like a zebra . . . Or spots. Leopards are quite handsome creatures. I wonder . . ."

Deep in thought, he put on his crown and then wandered through the door of his royal tent. Crossing the clearing was big, burly Bear carrying his fishing-rod.

"Hiya, Bear!" said the king. "I'd like a word with you."

"Good morning, Your Majesty," said Bear rather grumpily. He was late for fishing as it was.

"Tell me," said the king, "Does anyone do magic around here?"

Bear scratched his head. "Well, they do say that the Snake who lives in the coconut palm is a powerful spirit. Why don't you ask him?"

"Thank you, I will," said the king politely.

He went straight to the coconut palm. When he wanted something, he didn't believe in wasting time.

"Are you at home, Snake?" he roared.

There was a scurrying and a slithering among the leaves. Snake popped out his sleepy head. "Oh, Your M-m-majesty," he stammered. "Is there something wrong?"

The lion king cleared his throat. "Look here," he growled. "I'm tired of being this dull brown colour. I want to have spots like a leopard. I'm told you can help."

Now the Snake was really very annoyed at being disturbed like this. King or no king. He opened his sleepy eyes and hissed. "You must be tied tightly to the big baobab tree that stands in the middle of the jungle. Then wait and see what happens." The Snake slithered away, muttering angrily to himself.

The Lion king hurried down to the lagoon where bear was fishing. "Bear," he roared, "Come and tie me to the baobab tree."

Bear thought this was a very peculiar thing to do, but he didn't argue. After

all, you don't argue with a Lion king.

So, getting a thick strong rope, he wound it round and round the king and the baobab tree. He was feeling a bit annoyed, so he fastened it extra tightly.

"How's that, Your Majesty?" he asked.

"Fine. Fine," said the Lion king. "I can't move in the slightest."

By now all the other animals had heard what was happening. One by one they came to stare at the strange spectacle of their king tied to a baobab tree.

"I've never seen such a ridiculous thing," said Rhino.

"Quite incredible," said Crocodile.

"It's absolutely 'orrible," said Ostrich.

"Well, I'm going back to my fishing," said Bear.

The king waited and waited. But nothing happened. His legs were stiff with cramp but his skin did not change even a teeny weeny bit. He sighed. There was no sign of a spot. Not a single, solitary one.

The moon rose and shone over the jungle. The Lion king shivered. How he longed for his warm bed in the royal tent!

One by one the animals left, shaking their heads sadly.

It was a long, cold, miserable night for Lion. Dawn came and he was still a dull, brown colour.

All the animals crept back to stare in wonder at the king. The day passed and the second night. The second morning Bear brought the king some breakfast.

"Untie me," whispered the Lion hoarsely, his skin as brown as ever.

Bear undid the rope. "Are you all right, Your Majesty?"

"Of course," said the Lion, shaking his stiff, cold legs. "That was a special survival test, you know. We kings have to do one every so often just to show how strong we are."

And, roaring as majestically as he could, he stumbled off on his weak legs to the royal tent.

New Hair-Styles For The Ugly Sisters

DO YOU REMEMBER Cinderella's ugly selfish sisters? Well, this is a story about a very stupid thing they did one day.

You see, they had been invited out to dinner by the Mayor and were determined to look their very best. For, after all, some young men might be dining there, too, and they were anxious to make a good impression.

"I think I shall wear my red satin dress with the black stripes," said one of the ugly sisters.

"I think you're a little *too* fat to wear stripes," said the other ugly sister unkindly. "*I* shall wear my yellow velvet with the black spots."

"Yes, dear, it will go with the spots on your face," said her sister cruelly.

"And I must have my hair done in a very special way," said her sister, ignoring her remark. "I shall call in Monsieur Philippe to create a marvellous new fashion for me."

"So shall I!" said the other sister at once, for these two were very jealous of each other.

"Well, what style would you like, ladies?" asked Monsieur Philippe, twirling his comb and his long black moustache. It was the evening of the dinner party.

"Something fantastic!" said one ugly sister.

"Something stupendous!" said the other.

"Ah, let me see!" said Monsieur Philippe. He thought long and carefully. "Ah, I have it! A high pompadour fashion with tortoiseshell combs, and fine Spanish lace trailing behind."

"Too ordinary," said the first ugly sister.

"Too simple," said the second.

Monsieur Philippe thought again. "I have it!" he cried. "Bring me that birdcage with the canary inside."

The ugly sister brought the cage.

Monsieur Philippe perched it on her head, then he drew her hair up over the back and sides. The little bird peered between the bars. "Tweet! Tweet!" he cried in bewilderment.

Monsieur Philippe added a feather or two and then stepped back to admire his work, beaming with satisfaction. "Well, what do you think of that, madame?"

"Incredible!" cried the ugly sister. "Quite out of this world!"

"Oh, do mine! Do mine!" cried the second ugly sister impatiently.

Monsieur Philippe paced up and down the room, thinking hard. "Flowers? No, too obvious. Ah, I have it!" he cried, suddenly, staring at something which stood on the table.

It was the goldfish bowl in which swam a lively little goldfish.

Cleverly, Monsieur Philippe swept up the back hair. Then he perched the bowl on top of the ugly sister's head and arranged the hair neatly around it. He completed the effect with no less than five large combs. The goldfish swam round and round the bowl, with a most surprised look on his face.

"There, madame," Monsieur Philippe said, holding out a mirror.

The ugly sister smiled at her reflection.

"Superb," she said slowly. "Quite sensational!"

There was a clatter of horses' hooves and a sharp ring on the bell. The carriage had arrived.

Fussing and flurrying, the ugly sisters put on their jewels, picked up their bags, cloaks, gloves and fans, and then walked slowly and sedately out to the carriage.

Monsieur Philippe bowed politely. "You will look quite ravishing, ladies," he smiled. "No one will have a hair-style like yours."

When the carriage arrived at the Mayor's house, the coachman held open the door. Slowly, holding their heads as steady as they could, the two sisters got down from the carriage.

Suddenly the little canary burst into song. Tra-la-la-la-la!

How everyone stared!

Then the little goldfish started swimming frantically round and round his bowl, sloshing the water against the sides.

How everyone laughed!

The two ugly sisters looked at each other, their faces red with anger. And then something worse happened.

All the birds of the town flew around the ugly sister's head, trying to catch a glimpse of their little feathered friend, the canary.

And all the cats of the town crept up to stare greedily at the goldfish in his pond.

What confusion there was! The birds flapped their wings frantically. The cats mewed and began jumping up and down eagerly.

"Go away!" yelled the first ugly sister, trying to shoo away the birds.

CRASH! The bird-cage fell to the ground, the door burst open and away flew the canary.

"Stop it! Stop it!" yelled the second ugly sister, beating off the cats.

SPLOSH! The water from the fish-bowl splashed down her face. Quickly the coachman lifted off the bowl, just as it was about to fall.

Everyone laughed so much that tears ran down their faces. But the ugly sisters were crying in earnest.

"Home, coachman!" they screamed, getting back into the carriage.

So I'm afraid they didn't have dinner with the Mayor after all. But it was their own fault for being so vain.

Chip 'n' Dale Play a Trick On Grey Owl

IT HAD BEEN SNOWING hard all day in the forest, and the ground was covered with a thick layer of crisp, white snow.

Chip 'n' Dale worked very hard all afternoon, making a beautiful snowman near Big Oak where Mr. Grey Owl lived.

The snowman looked absolutely beautiful. And very real. Chip had found two shiny black stones for his eyes, and Dale had pressed in a small fir-cone for his nose.

The two little chipmunks danced up and down in excitement. But there was something missing. Suddenly Chip scampered off to his house in the tree. Soon he was back trailing a long woollen scarf behind him. He had found it in the woods last spring, and it was just what the snowman needed.

Carefully the two chipmunks tied the scarf around the snowman's neck. Then they stepped back to survey their master-piece. It was perfect.

The two chipmunks, chattering gaily, ran up the tree-trunk and knocked on Mr. Grey Owl's door.

"Who is it?" said a very sleepy voice. "It's Chip 'n' Dale, Mr. Grey Owl. You've got a visitor."

"Who is it?" asked Mr. Grey Owl, rather grumpily because he hated being woken up before it was dark.

"Don't know," said Chip, "But he looks a very important gentleman."

"I'll be down in a minute," said Mr. Grey Owl. "I'll just comb my feathers."

A few minutes later Mr. Grey Owl's front door opened. He flew down and

perched on a branch above the snowman.

"Good evening, sir," said Mr. Grey Owl, blinking his eyes short-sightedly. He couldn't see very clearly when it was still daylight. His eyesight was only sharp at night when he was looking for food. "What can I do for you?"

But the snowman didn't say a word.

Mr. Grey Owl cleared his throat nervously and began again. "I understand you want to see me," he said. "Is it anything important?"

But the snowman was completely silent.

"Perhaps he's shy," said Chip.

"Perhaps he's lost his tongue," said Dale.

"Perhaps his tongue is frozen," said Chip, giggling madly.

"Oh, I don't know," said Grey Owl puffing out his chest crossly. "I wish he'd state his business. I'm wasting valuable sleeping time."

"Well, I don't think this sort of man has any business," said Chip wisely.

"Only snow business," said Dale.

"*Snow* business?" said Grey Owl crossly. "What's that?"

"What *snowmen* have," said Chip 'n' Dale cheekily. And they laughed so much that they tumbled head-over-heels in the snow.

"Oh, you little rascals," said Grey Owl in his most scolding voice.

"Serve you right for telling us the moon was drowning in the pond," said Chip 'n' Dale, and giggling hysterically they scampered home through the snow.

Christopher Robin at The Circus

CHRISTOPHER ROBIN went to the Circus yesterday.

He *loves* the Circus. The lion act is one of his favourites. The lion-tamer was very brave. He locked himself in the cage with the fierce lions and he made them do all kinds of clever things.

But, best of all, Christopher Robin liked the clowns. They tumbled into the ring dressed like firemen with funny helmets on their heads. A little house in the middle of the ring was on fire and they tried to put out the flames.

They ran around the ring, trying to unwind the long water hoses, but they all got in each other's way and the hoses were all tangled up. Then they tried to put up the ladders, but they kept on falling down. At last they fixed the hoses to the water tap. They turned the taps on and the water came gushing out, but instead of pointing the hoses at the fire they pointed them at each other. Soon they were all soaking wet!

Then they left the hoses on the ground and began to pass buckets of water to each other. When the bucket reached the clown on the top of the ladder, instead of throwing the water on the fire he drank it! It was so funny . . .

"Are you glad you brought me?" Christopher Robin asked his father.

"Yes," said father. He was enjoying it as much as Christopher Robin!

Goofy Becomes a Footballer

ONE DAY MICKEY MOUSE met Goofy.

"Hello, Goofy," he said. "How are you?"

"I don't feel so good," said Goofy sadly. "I don't know what's the matter with me. But I feel so weak and tired."

"Why don't you take up a sport?" asked Mickey.

"A sport?" said Goofy in surprise. "What for? If you exercise, you will only feel weaker than ever!"

"That's not true," said Mickey. "Exercise is very good for you. In fact, to be really healthy you must play games. It's because you don't that you're ill."

"But I'm too old to play games," said Goofy.

"Nonsense," replied Mickey. "You're just lazy, that's all. Don't you know there are sports for every age?"

"No, I didn't know it," said Goofy. "What sport should I play?"

"You should ask your doctor," said Mickey. "He will tell you what is best."

A few weeks later, Mickey was walking by the park when he saw a figure dressed in bright blue shorts and a yellow shirt with red stripes. He looked a little familiar, but Mickey didn't know who it was. Suddenly the figure waved and kicked a football towards Mickey. It was Goofy!

"I hardly recognised you," said Mickey. "You look so healthy."

"I took your advice," said Goofy. "Now I'm captain of the football team!"

157

Lambert The Sheepish Lion

THE STORKS HAD WORKED hard all night delivering the baby animals to their mothers in the zoo. Now they were almost finished, but there was still one baby left. They were not sure who to give it to, but at last they decided it belonged to Mrs. Bleating, one of the sheep. But they had made a terrible mistake because the baby really belonged to the lions!

And that was how Lambert, the lion-cub, came to be brought up with the lambs.

Lambert grew quickly and soon he was huge. His mother was very happy to see her little child so strong, because, of course, no one ever doubted for a moment that Lambert really was a sheep.

Indeed, Lambert didn't behave at all like a lion. He was always gentle and shy like the other sheep. It never occurred to him that with a single blow he could knock down a tree. He was happy with the herd and loved to run and play as the other lambs did.

All the visitors to the zoo, men, women and children, could hardly believe their eyes when they saw such a fierce animal playing gently with the sheep. They were very worried that something might happen, but as soon as they saw that Lambert behaved like a real sheep they smiled. Lambert soon became the most popular animal in the zoo, it was such a fantastic sight to see such a wild beast living peacefully with the sheep.

One night a fierce wolf escaped from his cage. He crept towards the field where the sheep lived. Slowly the wolf

crept nearer and nearer. He was just about to spring on Lambert's mother when Lambert woke up.

Lambert was terrified to see such a fierce, ugly beast. He put his paws over his eyes and tried to hide. The wolf snarled and was just about to spring again when Lambert plucked up his courage. He couldn't let this wild beast eat his mother! With a great roar, Lambert hurled himself at the wolf!

It really was quite funny to see because Lambert had never attacked anyone before, and he did not know how to charge like a lion. He charged, butting his head at the wolf, just like a sheep!

But the wolf didn't like it. After all, Lambert *looked* like a lion; he looked like the fiercest, most savage lion in the zoo. The wolf moved back. Again Lambert threw himself headlong at the wolf. And again! And again!

The wolf decided that he had had enough. By now all the sheep were awake and they saw Lambert's brave deed. The wolf slunk away and he was so frightened that he never tried to attack the herd again.

How proud Mrs. Bleating was! Lambert was a hero! But the strange thing was that Lambert stayed as gentle as ever!

Alice In Wonderland

SOMETIMES WHEN WE ARE asleep all sorts of strange, exciting things happen to us. That's because we are dreaming. Alice was a great dreamer, and one hot afternoon when she fell asleep on the river bank this is what happened . . .

She saw a White Rabbit going along. He was looking at a watch which he had taken out of his waistcoat pocket. "Oh dear! Oh dear! I shall be late!" he cried.

Alice was very curious and so she followed him. But she fell down a deep well that seemed to go on for ever. But she wasn't hurt because she *floated* down ever so gently. At last she reached the bottom, and then many wonderful things happened to her and she saw many strange things which were similar and yet different from the world that she knew.

For instance, the beautiful flowers in the garden all had faces, and the rose and the white lily were very proud and treated the other poor flowers very badly.

On a little table Alice found a bottle with the words "DRINK ME" written on it. She decided to try it, and at once she began to grow, until she was as big as a giant. Then she drank from another bottle and began to shrink. Soon she was pleased to see that she was her proper size again.

In the forest Alice met all kinds of strange people. There was a caterpillar who sat on a mushroom smoking a pipe, and a Cheshire cat who had a wonderful grin but who kept on appearing and disappearing.

Then Alice met a Mad Hatter, a March Hare and a Dormouse who were having a tea-party. The Mad Hatter was quite crazy. He wore a shiny top-hat and

he used to celebrate his "Un-Birthdays", so that he had a party every day of the year except one!

The Dormouse told a silly story and then the March Hare and the Mad Hatter put him in the teapot where he fell fast asleep!

Then Alice met some gardeners who looked like playing-cards. They were painting the roses on the bushes red because the Queen didn't like white roses.

Then a great procession came by led by the White Rabbit blowing a trumpet. Behind him came the Queen of the country and her soldiers. She was very fat and very, very unkind to all her subjects. To Alice's surprise, she was a playing-card, too.

The Queen didn't like the look of Alice. "Off with her head!" she cried.

"Why, you're nothing but a pack of cards," said Alice angrily. And the whole pack of cards rose up and flew at her.

It was then that Alice woke up.

"Why, it was only a dream!" she said in surprise.

Isn't it a pity that the things that happen in dreams don't really happen?

Have *you* ever had an exciting dream?

The Grasshopper And The Ants

THE MERRY NOTES of the violin which the grasshopper was playing floated on the air and reached the place where the ants were busy collecting food.

"It's the grasshopper again!" they said. "He's always playing that violin of his. He never seems to do any work."

Just then the grasshopper danced by. He stopped when he saw the ants. "Why are you working on such a beautiful day?" he asked. "Don't you feel the gaiety of spring? Why aren't you dancing and singing?"

"We must collect our food now," said the queen of the ants. "If we don't, what will we do when winter comes?"

"Oh, winter is a long way off," said the grasshopper. "You take life much too seriously."

"But you must work today if you want to eat tomorrow," said the queen of the ants. "You can play the violin when you've finished," said the little ants as they scurried about.

The ants were really being very sensible but the grasshopper didn't want to take their wise advice.

"Go on with your work, my little friends," he said. "I'm going to dance in the meadow in the sunshine." And so the grasshopper left the busy ants and went on his way, singing.

The spring soon passed, and the warm days of summer came. All day long the

grasshopper lazily sat in the sun, or slept on a blade of grass, or played his violin in the shade of the poppies.

But the summer was soon over. The days began to get colder. The leaves dropped from the trees and many of the animals began their winter sleep.

One morning, when the grasshopper woke up, he was surprised to see that snow had fallen during the night. He shivered and pulled his scarf tightly around his neck.

"I'd better go and look for something to eat," he said.

But although he searched and searched, he could not find a thing. The meadow was covered with a thick carpet of snow and the ground underneath was as hard as iron.

"Oh dear! Oh dear! What shall I do?"

cried the grasshopper. "I shall die of hunger! I shall freeze to death!"

The grasshopper wandered around looking for somewhere to hide. But he couldn't find a warm place anywhere.

"Oh dear! Oh dear!" he sighed. "How silly I was not to listen to the ants. While I am dying of cold and hunger they are sitting in a nice warm house with lots of good things to eat."

And, sobbing loudly, the grasshopper sat down in the snow.

The ants heard his sad cry and as they were really very kind creatures they came hurrying to help him. By this time the poor grasshopper was frozen stiff. The ants picked him up and carried him back to their nest.

The grasshopper felt better, and never forgot the lesson he had been taught.

Duchess And The Catnapper

DUCHESS LOOKED AROUND her and purred contentedly. What an exciting scene it was! The great hall in the centre of Paris was full of cats and their proud owners. There was every kind of cat imaginable —sly Siamese, haughty Abyssinians, timid Tortoiseshells, Ginger Marmalades, and even common Tabbies. There was a sprinkling of fluffy Persians, like Duchess herself, but not one that was as truly aristocatic.

It was the day of the great Paris Cat Show. Duchess settled herself comfortably on her blue silk cushion in her wickerwork cage. Then she lazily yawned and licked her beautifully-manicured paw. Madame Bonfamille had brushed her coat until the fur was as smooth as silk, and perched pertly on the top of her head was a spotted pink bow.

Duchess looked a picture. She was the handsomest cat in the whole show. And she knew it. And her kittens, Marie, Berlioz and Toulouse, watching her proudly, knew it. And Thomas O'Malley knew it. And Scat Cat and all his cool cat friends. They only hoped the judges knew it, for everyone wanted Duchess to win the silver cup.

"There, my beauty," said Madame Bonfamille, stroking her softly through the bars of the basket, "We'll all leave you for a moment so that you can rest. It will be your turn, soon."

So Madame Bonfamille, the three kittens, and all their friends went off to watch the judging of the Siamese cats.

Duchess yawned again. She really did feel sleepy. It was very hot in the hall because of the big blazing lights, and quite noisy. She turned round daintily and, curving her beautiful bushy tail around her, she lay on her cushion and closed her eyes. Hmm! That was better . . .

Soon Duchess was asleep, dreaming of a big saucer of rich creamy milk. She was about to lap it up, but instead of cool liquid she felt something rough and nasty-tasting in her mouth.

Duchess opened her eyes. At once she was terribly frightened, because she couldn't see! Instead of the bright lights of the hall she was surrounded by gloomy darkness.

She was in a sack!

Help! Help!" she cried, struggling with all her might.

She felt herself lifted up into the air.

"Help! Oh help!" she screamed, fighting furiously.

Although she was terrified, she knew exactly what was happening. She was being kidnapped, which wasn't really so surprising. She was, after all, the most aristocatic and expensive cat in the show. But Duchess was brave, too, and she wasn't going to give in without a struggle.

She slashed at the sack with her strong claws until she had made a hole.

"Save me! Save me!" she screamed as loud as she could.

Thomas O'Malley heard her.

"Someone is stealing a cat!" he cried

excitedly and bounded over to where the noise was coming from.

Then he saw Duchess's cage—EMPTY!

"It's Duchess!" he yelled excitedly. "Come on, cats, after him!"

By this time Madame Bonfamille had realised what had happened. "Stop thief! Stop thief!" she cried, hastily picking up the three kittens to prevent them being trampled on in the rush.

What confusion there was then!

The cat-thief stopped, the sack with the struggling Duchess inside dangling from his hand. The door was guarded—the open window was his only chance. He turned towards it, and was about to leap upwards but—

Too late!

Around him swarmed a horde of angry cats. All of Thomas O'Malley's and Scat Cat's friends had come to the rescue. And there's nothing as angry as a cool cat when it's roused.

Spitting and snarling, they jumped up the cat-thief's legs, tearing at his trousers. Some sprang on to his shoulders and lashed out at his face.

Screaming, he put up his hands to protect himself, and dropped the sack. At once Madame Bonfamille snatched it up and opened it. Seconds later she was stroking and comforting a very upset Duchess.

But the cats hadn't finished with the cat-thief.

They had him down on the floor now, and swarmed all over him.

"Help! Help!" he pleaded, his face and hands covered with deep red scratches.

"That's enough, cats!" cried Madame Bonfamille. "I think he's learned his lesson!"

The cats jumped down and squatted on their haunches in a ring around the cat-thief, staring at him with cold, pitiless eyes.

He was glad when the police led him away in handcuffs.

"That was Pierre, the famous Cat-napper," said one of the judges. "I don't think he will ever try his tricks again."

Duchess was soon her old elegant self again. "This is a day I'll never forget," she purred.

And she never did. For guess who won the first prize for the best champion cat of all?

Why, Duchess of course!

Lost In The Fog

ONE NIGHT, in the very middle of winter, Rat woke up. He looked around his comfortable little underground room and rubbed his eyes. He felt that he had been sleeping a long, long time. "I wonder if spring has come?" he said to himself.

He got out of bed and put on a thick overcoat. "I think I'll just take a little look outside."

He popped his head out of his hole in the river bank. It was very dark and very quiet. Every creature in the world must be fast asleep.

"I'd better go back, I suppose," he sighed. "But I wish I knew when spring was coming."

He was just about to return to his little warm room when he suddenly thought, "Why not ask Mole? He will know how many weeks there are till spring."

Rat jumped out of his hole and buttoned up his overcoat. A chilly wind was blowing and he felt very cold.

"Now, let me see," he said to himself, as he hurried along. "Straight down to the willow-tree, turn left until I reach the clump of rushes, then right until I reach the meadow."

Off he scurried down the path. It was so dark that he could hardly see. He had just passed the willow-tree when suddenly a thick cloud seemed to float down around him. It was a strange yellow colour, like smoke, and it made him cough and splutter.

"This must be the terrible fog I've heard about," he said. "Oh dear, I'd better go back."

He turned round quickly and hurried back the way he had come. The fog was so dense now that when he held up his paw in front of his face he couldn't see it!

"Oh dear! Oh dear! Where is the willow-tree?" he cried. Then he stumbled over a stone and nearly fell over. "Oh dear! Where is the path?" he cried, quite terrified, for by now he had realised the terrible fact that HE WAS LOST!

He sat down, just where he was, and put his head in his paws. What a fool he had been to leave his snug little house.

He lifted up his head and looked all around him at the thick yellow fog. What was he to do? He couldn't stay there all night. He would freeze . . .

Suddenly, ahead of him, he saw a little twinkling light. It was a tiny glow-worm.

"Come on," said the glow-worm. "I'll take you home. Just follow me."

So Rat followed the tiny light, past the willow-tree, along the river bank, until the glow-worm stopped.

"There, Ratty, there's your house. Now, go back to sleep."

"Thank you, thank you," cried Ratty. But the little twinkling light was gone.

Rat took off his overcoat and climbed back into his cosy bed. Soon he was fast asleep. He was so glad to be back that he slept soundly until the first day of spring when he was woken up by Mole tapping loudly on his front door!

King Arthur Risks His Life

THIS IS A STORY about Arthur who, long, long ago, was King of England.

Soon after Aurther had been made King, one of his knights was killed and another badly wounded by a fierce knight who lived by a well deep in the forest.

Arthur was very angry about this, and one day he put on his armour and rode out to meet this knight.

On the way he met Merlin, the powerful wizard. "Don't go into the forest," warned Merlin. "That knight is very dangerous."

But Arthur was determined. Merlin rode with him until they reached the the well. A rich pavilion stood by the well and outside it an armed knight was waiting.

"Sir knight," said Arthur, "Why do you wait here so that no one can ride past without fighting you?"

"Because I want to," answered the knight boldly. "And if anyone doesn't like it, they're welcome to try and stop me."

"I'll stop you!" cried Arthur bravely.

"We'll see about that!" said the knight, and he mounted his horse and prepared to do battle.

They charged each other, and each hit the other in the middle of his shield, so hard that both spears split in two, right down the middle!

At once, Arthur pulled out his sword.

"No," said the strange knight, "it's fairer that we fight with spears." His squire brought two new spears and the knights again charged each other.

This time they charged so furiously that both the spears broke exactly in half.

Once more Arthur put his hand to his sword, but the knight called out, "You're the best jouster I've ever met. Let's try again."

"Agreed," said Arthur.

Two more great spears were brought. Each knight took one and charged furiously. This time Arthur's spear hit the knight's shield and broke into pieces. At once the knight hit Arthur's shield so hard that Arthur and his horse fell to the ground.

The King leapt up and drew his sword. Immediately the knight got off his horse, and they continued the battle on foot.

They fought for a long time, their

swords flashing through the air. They both became so breathless that they had to rest for a while. Then they went to battle again. At last their swords met with a great CLANG!

And Arthur's sword broke into two pieces!

The strange knight cried, "Now you are in my power. I can save you or kill you. Unless you agree that I am the victor, you shall die."

"Never!" cried Arthur. And he leapt at the knight, caught hold of him round the middle and threw him to the ground. But the knight, who was very big and strong, jumped up at Arthur and knocked him over, pinning him to the ground. He pulled off the King's helmet and was going to cut off his head . . .

"Stop!" cried Merlin. "If you kill that knight you will put the whole of England in danger."

"Why, who is he?" asked the knight in surprise.

"He is King Arthur," said Merlin.

The knight was so ashamed that he lifted up his sword to kill himself. But Merlin cast a spell on him so that he fell down as though asleep.

"Alas!" cried Arthur. "Have you killed this great fighter with your magic?"

"Don't worry," said Merlin. "He will awake within three hours. His name is Sir Pellinore, and he is a great knight. He and his two sons will serve you well."

And indeed Sir Pellinore and his sons became King Arthur's loyal and trusted knights.

The Birthday Party

IT WAS NEARLY TIME for bed. Berlioz, Marie and Toulouse, the aristocatic kittens, were washing their faces in front of the fire. At least, they SHOULD have been washing their faces but they were much too excited. Tomorrow was their birthday.

"Do you think we'll get any presents?" said Marie, in a dreamy sort of voice.

Berlioz stopped washing his whiskers. "Oh, I should think so. *Everyone* gets presents on their birthday."

"Perhaps we won't," said Toulouse suddenly. "Perhaps nobody *knows* it is our birthday."

The three little kittens looked at each other sadly. They hadn't thought of *that*!

"Oh well!" mewed Berlioz. "It's too late now. We can't *tell* everybody." So rather miserably the three kittens curled up in their basket and went to sleep.

Marie was the first to wake up. At least, she opened one eye and looked around. There was not a present in sight.

Soon Duchess, their mother, came along.

"Come along, kittens. Time for breakfast," she said briskly.

The kittens followed her sadly to the kitchen. Their friend Thomas O'Malley was lapping his milk. "Good morning, Kittikins," he called gaily. "Lovely day."

Silently the kittens lapped their milk. They were much too polite and aristocatic to remind Duchess and O'Malley that it was their birthday. Duchess ought to know, anyway. After all, she was their mother. But she didn't say a word.

"Now, run along, dears," she said when the kittens had finished. "I must have a word with O'Malley."

Sadly the kittens went upstairs to the drawing-room. Perhaps Madame Bonfamille had a present for them.

"Hello, my beauties," said Madame cheerfully. But there was no sign of a present.

Marie sat sadly on her favourite chair and blinked back a tear. Berlioz and Toulouse tried hard to behave like grown-up cats. But what a miserable birthday it was.

It was after tea that it happened. The three kittens were dozing in front of the fire when they were suddenly awakened by the tinkling notes of the piano. The cheerful notes of "Happy Birthday to You" echoed around the room. It was Scat Cat!

Suddenly the room seemed full of cats! Aristocatic cats, alley cats, ever-so-cool cats. And each one carried a present!

"Happy Birthday, darlings!" cried Duchess, giving each of her kittens a furry little kiss.

"Did you think we'd forgotten?" said O'Malley. "As if we would!"

"We wanted to surprise you," said Duchess with a smile.

And what a surprise it was! The kittens could hardly believe their eyes!

A pretty tablecloth was laid on the carpet and on it were arranged saucers of every kind of delicacy imaginable—salmon, caviar, thick cream, fish-pie, jellied eels. All the food that cats adore!

And you should have seen the presents! Jewel-studded collars, and pretty bells, silk cushions to lie on, combs and mirrors . . .

"Oh, how lovely!" cried the little kittens, their faces beaming with delight.

Scat Cat and his musicians struck up a merry tune. And everyone danced till dawn! The party is still the talk of Paris!

Daisy Bakes A Cake

IT WAS DONALD DUCK'S birthday and Daisy Duck, his girl-friend, was making him a cake. It was a very rich cake, full of all kinds of fruit, and Daisy stirred it briskly. Then she popped it into the oven.

A few hours later she took it out. Mmm! Mmm! It smelt delicious. Daisy put the cake into the cupboard to cool. She would decorate it later when she came back from the hairdresser's She had to look beautiful that night: Donald was taking her out to a very special dinner.

Hours later, Daisy returned, her hair all prettily waved and curled. She iced the cake and put "HAPPY BIRTHDAY DONALD" on it in big pink letters.

Then quickly she flew upstairs to change into a party dress. Donald would soon be calling.

Ting-a-ling! Ting-a-ling!

Donald rang Daisy's front door bell.

No one answered.

Ting-a-ling! Ting-a-ling!

No reply. Donald put his finger on the bell and leaned hard on it.

Ting-a-ling-ling-ling-ling-ling-ling!

At last the door opened. It was Daisy. And she was crying.

"It's about time!" said Donald, and stopped. He had seen Daisy's tears. "What is it?" he asked. "Is this the way to greet a handsome duck on his birthday?"

"Oh Donald!" said Daisy miserably. "Something terrible has happened."

"Tell me the worst," said Donald. "What is it now?"

"Oh Donald!" moaned Daisy. "I've lost your engagement ring!"

"Quack! Quack!" said Donald, very upset. This was indeed a sad business. Daisy's engagement ring was a lovely sparkling diamond and it had cost Donald a lot of money. Most of his savings, in fact.

"Oh dear, Daisy!" he quacked. "Have you looked everywhere?"

"Everywhere," said Daisy in a forlorn little voice. "All over the kitchen and the sitting-room and the bedroom. I've

"Well, it's no good crying," said Donald. "Let's look again." So together, Donald and Daisy searched every nook and cranny of the house.

There was no sign of the ring.

"Well, that's that," sighed Donald. "Goodbye diamond ring."

"Oh Donald," cried Daisy. "I've spoilt your birthday. And I made you such a beautiful birthday cake, too."

"Well, I'll have a bit of it now," said Donald miserably. "I feel much too tired after all that searching to go out to dinner."

Daisy wiped her eyes and bravely tried to smile. "I'll save up, Donald," she said. "I'll save up every penny and give it to you."

"Yes," said Donald, "so that I can buy a ring for you to lose again."

"Boo! Hoo! Boo! Hoo!" Daisy had burst into tears again.

Donald patted her gently on the back. "Sorry, old girl," he said. "That was mean of me. You couldn't *help* losing it. How about some of that birthday cake, eh?"

crawled over every bit of the carpet."

"Where did you go today?" asked Donald, trying to be sensible.

"To the hairdresser's," said Daisy. "I've just rung them but there's no sign of it."

"Were you wearing it today?" said Donald.

"Oh yes," said Daisy, wiping her eyes with a dainty lace handkerchief. "I *always* wear it. It's so beautiful."

Daisy went to the cupboard and got the cake. It looked wonderful. She cut a great big slice, and putting it on a plate gave it to Donald. Then she poured two glasses of wine.

"Happy birthday, Donald," said Daisy, gulping down a sob.

"Ah! scrumptious!" said Donald, biting into the cake.

Suddenly he stopped chewing. His face wrinkled into a frown. Putting up a hand he took something from his mouth. "That was a pretty hard currant," he cried, putting it down on his plate. There was a faint tinkle . . .

Daisy darted forward. "That's no currant, Donald," she cried excitedly. "It's my engagement ring!"

And indeed it was! "Quack! Quack!" cried Donald joyfully.

"It must have fallen into the mixture when I baked the cake," quacked Daisy, unable to believe her eyes.

"Come on, sweetheart," cried Donald merrily, "Get your coat. We're off to that celebration dinner. Quack! Quack!"

The Sleep Walking Pelican

ON A NEST right at the top of a lighthouse lived a pelican and a little woodpecker. The two of them were very good friends and they had lived together a long time. But the little woodpecker was rather worried. His friend the pelican had a very bad and dangerous habit. He used to walk in his sleep!

Every night, as soon as he was asleep, the pelican flew away from the nest and down over the sea. Every time he did this his life was in danger because many times he was almost eaten by the sharks. The woodpecker was afraid, too, that one night he would fly so far away that he would never find his way back.

The little woodpecker didn't know what to do. He tried to keep his friend awake, but of course the pelican became so tired that he soon dropped off. As soon as he did, off he flew into danger.

The woodpecker thought and thought about the problem, until, at last, he thought he had found the answer.

He tied a heavy anchor to the pelican's leg.

"That should stop the night-flying," he said to himself.

But that night the sleeping pelican tried to fly again, and the weight of the anchor dragged him down to the bottom of the sea. He almost drowned! But the cold water woke up the pelican and he managed to free himself from the anchor.

The pelican was very angry with the woodpecker, but to tell the truth his anger did not last long because he knew that his friend was only trying to help.

The woodpecker went on thinking about the problem.

"There must be an answer somewhere," he said to himself.

At last he had a brilliant idea.

"That's it!" he cried. "The very thing."

That night when the pelican went to bed the woodpecker tied a strong rope around his leg and fastened the other end to the weather-vane on the top of the lighthouse.

Soon the pelican was asleep. As usual it was not long before he flapped his wings and took off. But as he was tied to the weather-vane he could not fall into the sea, and he could not fly far away. Now there was no risk of his drowning or of being lost.

Round and round the lighthouse the pelican flew! Fast asleep! And safe!

Now the woodpecker ties the pelican to the weather-vane every night. The two friends sleep peacefully at last—the woodpecker in his warm bed and the pelican travelling round the lighthouse!

G.B.S. — M

The Little Red Hen

ONE DAY, as she was walking along the lane, the little red hen found a grain of wheat. She picked it up and put it in her basket. "I will plant it," she said. "Perhaps it will grow and when it is harvest-time I will make bread with it."

As she walked along, she met Donald Duck's three little nephews.

"Will you help me to plant this grain of wheat?" she asked them politely.

"Oh, we can't!" said the little ducks. "We are much too busy playing."

Her friends in the farmyard couldn't help either, so the little red hen had to do it by herself.

The months passed by and the little grain of wheat grew and grew. Soon the little red hen had a lovely crop and it was just the right time to cut it down.

She went to her friends in the farm-yard and asked them, "Who will help me to harvest my wheat?"

But all the other chickens only said, "Cluck! Cluck! We are having a rest. It's much too hot to work in the fields."

So the little red hen cut all the wheat by herself. She worked all the afternoon and the evening in the hot sun until all the wheat was cut down. Then she tied it into neat bundles. By this time it was almost dark, and the little red hen felt very tired.

Some days later she asked her friends if they would help her to carry the wheat to the mill to be ground into flour.

"Cluck! Cluck!" said the chickens

crossly. "Go away and stop bothering us!"

So the little red hen carried the wheat to the mill all by herself.

A few months later the little red hen said to the chickens, "Would anyone like some of my flour to bake bread?"

But once more the lazy chickens didn't want to work. "Go away!" they said. "We don't feel like making bread."

So the little red hen went back to her kitchen. She made some lovely crusty loaves and some marvellous pies, and popped them in the oven to bake.

When she opened the oven later a most delicious aroma floated into the kitchen. It floated out through the door and windows and down to the yard where the lazy chickens were sitting, feeling rather hungry.

"What's that wonderful smell?" they asked, clucking furiously. "It's coming from the little red hen's house. Let's go and see!"

So all the chickens hurried to the house and looked through the window. When they saw the lovely bread and pies, they cried, "Oh, please give us a little bit!"

"Certainly not!" said the little red hen. "I asked you to help me plant the wheat, reap it, grind it and knead it, but you wouldn't. I had to do it all by myself. I can eat it by myself, too!"

And the little red hen cut a slice of pie and began to eat it.

The chickens couldn't bear to look at her. They all crept away, covering their noses so that they couldn't smell the delicious smell!

The Gentle Dragon

ON THE LAST STONE of the village there stood a notice on which these terrible words were painted, "Beware! There is a dragon in the neighbourhood."

Now, no one had ever seen this dragon, but everyone was afraid of him. Every single person who lived in the village. No . . . not *everyone*. There was one person who thought it would be wonderful to see a dragon, a real live dragon of flesh and blood.

Do you know who this brave person was?

A child like you.

One day he set off towards the dragon's den. When he reached it, he saw the dragon sitting outside. He was a huge beast, just as the stories had said, but the boy was surprised to see that the dragon was quietly reading a book! In fact, the dragon seemed a very peaceful dragon. There weren't even flames coming from his nostrils!

"But you're not at all fierce!" said the boy in wonder.

"Oh no!" said the dragon. "To tell the truth, I'm a poet. I'm not interested in carrying off princesses or fighting battles with knights in armour."

The dragon was very glad to have a

180

visitor and he and the boy soon became good friends.

But the notice attracted many people to the outskirts of the village. One day a knight rode up, armed with a lance and sword.

"I'm ready to fight the dragon!" he cried.

"Good!" cried the people, because they wanted the dragon to be killed.

The boy was very worried. How could he stop the knight and the dragon from fighting?

When the knight was riding to the dragon's den, the boy suddenly ran in front of his horse.

"Stop!" he cried. "The dragon doesn't want to fight! He's a gentle, peaceful dragon!"

The knight didn't know what to do. He got down from his horse and took off his helmet. The boy could see then that he, too, had a very kind face.

"To tell the truth," he said, "I don't want to fight much, either. What shall we do?"

At last they decided to visit the dragon to see if they could find the solution to the problem.

The knight was delighted to meet the dragon, because he was a poet too and he understood perfectly how the dragon felt. At last they decided to *pretend* to fight and the dragon *pretend* to be killed. And so everything ended well . . .

But it wasn't really the end. The villagers found out. For a few months later some wild beasts began to terrorise the village. The dragon came down from his den and drove them away. How glad the villagers were that the dragon was still alive! And how pleased they were to have such a good neighbour!

And so the poetic dragon went on living there for many years, happy and contented, writing the most beautiful poetry.

Jiminy Cricket

"HELLO, LITTLE FRIENDS!

"Do you remember me?

"My name is Jiminy Cricket and I'm Pinocchio's conscience.

"The Blue Fairy has asked me to look after the little wooden puppet. I help him choose between right and wrong.

"It's a very important job and sometimes it's rather difficult. But although I'm very small, I really am very experienced. I've travelled all over the world and met all sorts of people. I go everywhere with Pinocchio, to make sure that he doesn't get into trouble.

"Of course, little boys often get into trouble. Sometimes it's not their fault.

Sometimes wicked older boys lead them astray.

"Whenever Pinocchio feels that perhaps he might do something wrong, he gives a little whistle and then I rush to help him. It's a sort of secret code.

"Whenever *you* feel you might do something wrong, *you* should give a little whistle, and then perhaps you won't do anything silly after all.

"Just remember this little song:
When you can't tell right from wrong
Give a little whistle!
Give a little whistle!
And always let your conscience be your guide."

Bambi Finds A Playmate

BAMBI, THE PRINCE of the Forest, couldn't find anybody to play with. Of course, they would have played with the fawn if they had been *there* to play with him.

But they weren't. They were at school.

And if you ask why Bambi wasn't at school it is because he had caught a chill and was only now getting over it. His mother had kept him snug and warm until he was better and ol' Doc Owl had prescribed some nasty medicine.

So now Bambi was feeling better. And Doc Owl had said he could go out and play and then go back to school tomorrow.

But *today* he had nobody to play with. What do you do if you are by yourself? Count the leaves on the trees? Count the clouds in the sky?

Count yourself unhappy because you've nobody to play with?

Bambi did all three and was feeling very lonely when he heard the noise:

"Thump! Thump!"

"Thump! Thump!"

Bambi knew who that was. His old friend, Thumper Rabbit, who beat the ground with his hind feet. Eagerly Bambi ran to where the noise was coming from.

It *was* Thumper.

"Hello, Thumper, what are you doing out of school?"

Thumper laughed: "I've had a chill, but now I'm better. But I've nobody to play with."

Bambi laughed: "Same here."

So they played together. And the Prince of the Forest was not lonely any more.

The Sword of The Lake

DO YOU REMEMBER the story of Wart, the adopted son of Sir Ector, who became the famous King Arthur?

One day, soon after he had become King, Arthur said to Merlin, the powerful wizard, "I have no sword; and a king should have a sword."

"There is a sword nearby," said Merlin mysteriously. "And it shall be yours if you can get it."

So they rode together to a beautiful, broad lake.

In the middle of the lake, Arthur saw an arm rise out of the water dressed in rich silk. In its hand was a beautiful gleaming sword!

"Look," said Merlin. "There is the sword I told you about."

Suddenly they saw a lovely maiden walking by the lake.

"Who is that?" whispered Arthur.

"She is the Lady of the Lake," said Merlin. "She will come and speak to you. Talk politely and gently to her, then she will give you the sword."

The maiden came nearer to Arthur

and they greeted each other.

"Sweet maiden," said Arthur softly, "What sword is that the arm holds above the water? I wish it were mine, for I have no sword."

"King Arthur," said the maiden, "that sword is mine. It is called Excalibur. You shall have it. Go into the barge that you see there, and row yourself to the sword. Take it and the scabbard with you."

So Arthur got down from his horse and tied him to a tree. He stepped on to the barge and rowed out to the middle of the lake.

When he came to the sword that the hand held, he grasped it by the hilt and lifted it up. At once the arm in its rich sleeve of silk sank into the water and not a sign of it was seen.

Arthur rowed back to the shore where Merlin was waiting. The beautiful maiden had vanished.

Arthur and Merlin mounted their horses again and rode away, King Arthur clutching the sword proudly.

King Arthur always carried his sword, Excalibur, and it served him faithfully.

When at the end of a long and glorious reign, King Arthur was dying he called to him his most trusted knight, Sir Bedivere.

"Take Excalibur," said Arthur, "and throw it back into the lake."

But Sir Bedivere hated to throw the noble sword away. He took it and hid it. Then he returned to the King.

"Did you throw Excalibur into the lake?" asked Arthur.

"Yes, Sire," said Sir Bedivere.

"What did you see?" asked the King.

"Sire," he replied, "nothing but the wind and the waves."

King Arthur knew then that Sir Bedivere was lying. He sent him again to the lake.

But once more Sir Bedivere could not bear to throw away the famous sword. He returned to the King, pretending that he had.

"What did you see this time?" asked Arthur.

"The sword sank into the water," said

185

Sir Bedivere.

The King flew into a terrible rage. He could see that Sir Bedivere was still lying.

"Throw it in at once!" he cried in a terrible voice. "I am your King and I command you!"

This time Sir Bedivere did what he was told.

He took the beautiful sword from its hiding-place and went to the lake. He held the sword by the hilt and then threw it as far as he could out into the water.

To his astonishment an arm and a hand came out of the water. The hand grasped Excalibur, waved it three times and vanished.

Sir Bedivere hurried back to King Arthur and told him what he had seen. The King was satisfied this time and knew that Sir Bedivere was telling the truth.

He also knew that it was time for him, too, to leave the world. He asked Sir Bedivere to help him to the water's side.

There a barge was waiting. In it sat many ladies dressed in black.

They took King Arthur and made him comfortable in the stern of the barge.

The barge moved gently over the lake.

Sir Bedivere watched sadly as the great and noble King Arthur sailed away. He was never seen again, but the memory of his great and noble deeds will live forever.

Pluto Gives Father Christmas A Helping Hand

IT WAS CHRISTMAS EVE and the snow was falling thick and fast. The north wind howled down the chimney. But it was warm and cosy in Mickey Mouse's house. Mickey sat in his favourite armchair, in front of a roaring fire, a biscuit in one hand and a glass of milk in the other.

Pluto lay on the rug in front of the fire, watching the dancing flames and dreaming of juicy steaks.

"Ah, this is the life, Pluto," sighed Mickey. "I'm sorry for all those folks who have to be out on a night like this."

Suddenly there was a rat-tat-tat on the door.

Pluto cocked up his ears. Who could be calling at this time of night?

Mickey Mouse went to the door and opened it.

Who do you think stood there in a cloud of twirling snow?

Why, Father Christmas himself!

"Sorry to bother you," he said, "but I really am in a most frightful mess."

"What is it?" asked Mickey in surprise.

"It's my reindeer," said Father Christmas sadly. "They've all caught the 'flu. I've had to take them back home and tuck them up in bed. And here I am with lots more toys to deliver. Oh dear! Oh dear! What shall I do?"

"That *is* a problem," said Mickey. "What can we do?" and he looked anxiously at Pluto.

"Woof! Woof!" said Pluto sympathetically.

"My sleigh is outside," said Father Christmas. "All loaded up with toys. There's only a few more villages left to to visit. The children will be so disappointed."

"It's really too sad," said Mickey, shaking his head. "If I had a horse I'd gladly lend him to you. But I've only got Pluto."

PLUTO!!

Mickey turned and looked at Pluto, who was still lying by the fire.

"He's a good strong dog," said Mickey thoughtfully. "Do you think he could pull your sleigh?"

Father Christmas came into the room and looked at Pluto.

"Stand up, Pluto!" ordered Mickey. "Let Father Christmas have a good look at you."

Pluto looked at Mickey in astonishment and rather unwillingly got to his feet. What a thing to suggest! As if *he* could pull a sleigh!

"He's a fine dog," said Father Christmas. "I'm sure he could do it."

"What a great honour for you, Pluto," said Mickey. "To be allowed to pull Father Christmas's sleigh!"

Pluto barked proudly. Come to think of it, it really was something rather special. His friends would be jealous!

Quickly Father Christmas and Micky harnessed Pluto to the sleigh. "Can I come too?" asked Mickey. "I could give you a hand, and we'd get it done much quicker."

"With pleasure," said Father Christmas, who was a very friendly and polite old man.

So Father Christmas picked up the reins and Mickey jumped on behind.

"Gee up!" yelled Father Christmas. "Woof!" barked Pluto.

They were off! The sleigh-bells tinkling merrily, Pluto trotted off through the snow. It was all great fun and Pluto and Mickey enjoyed it immensely.

The children enjoyed opening their presents on Christmas morning, too. But little did they know that it was Pluto and Mickey Mouse who had helped Father Christmas bring them!

Goofy In The Wild West

"HELLO, MY LITTLE FRIENDS! How's life? You weren't expecting to see me dressed like this, were you?

"Well, the fact is, your old friend Goofy is now a fantastic cowboy.

"Look how I'm dressed. Look carefully. I haven't forgotten a single thing, have it?

"Trousers of the finest leather, tall boots with high heels and silver spurs, a big white cowboy hat, a red kerchief round my neck, a broad belt with lots of bullets, and last but not least two shining, evil-looking pistols.

"I'm a splendid sight, aren't I?

"You should see me galloping over the prairies, fearlessly capturing all the bandits that dare to cross my path.

"The day will soon come when they'll give me my nickname. They'll call me Goofy Kid.

"It's a fine name, isn't it? Hasn't it got a wonderful ring? Goofy Kid!

"I shall be a great hero. They might even make me Sheriff. For I intend to capture the greatest bandit of all—One-Eyed Jack.

"Of course, there are still one or two things I have to learn, like how to ride a horse, how to throw a lassoo, and how to fire a gun. But these are little things and not very important.

"I *look* wonderful, and that's the main thing. Don't you agree, little friends?